CHALLENGING LOVE

Keith Chilton was a shy young man. Dedicated to tracing a disease that had killed off a beloved relative, he valued the peace and security of his laboratory and the use of the library in his uncle's house. Then his uncle died and bequeathed the house and library to Keith provided he got himself married. Overcoming his reluctance, he began to meet likely young women . . . only to fall in love with the mysterious Rachel Beamish, his grey-haired, severe, bespectacled secretary . . .

Books by Eileen Barry
in the Linford Romance Library:

THE REDUNDANT HEART

EILEEN BARRY

CHALLENGING LOVE

Complete and Unabridged

LINFORD
Leicester

First published in Great Britain in 1976

First Linford Edition
published 2010

British Library CIP Data

Barry, Eileen.
  Challenging love. - -
  (Linford romance library)
  1. Inheritance and succession- -Fiction.
  2. Medicine- -Research- -Fiction.
  3. Secretaries- -Fiction. 4. Love stories.
  5. Large type books.
  I. Title II. Series
  823.9'14–dc22

  ISBN 978–1–44480–071–5

Published by
F. A. Thorpe (Publishing)
Anstey, Leicestershire

Set by Words & Graphics Ltd.
Anstey, Leicestershire
Printed and bound in Great Britain by
T. J. International Ltd., Padstow, Cornwall

This book is printed on acid-free paper

1

'I never thought he'd do this to me. Not him!' Keith Chilton stood at the end of the great library at Chilton Grange, staring out at the dripping vista. In spite of the rain, it was an incredibly beautiful view. The gardens had been landscaped specially for old Edward Chilton's grandfather. In fact, more money had poured into the grounds and the surrounding estate than into the house. All the Chiltons had been outdoor men, until Keith himself had come home from the Tropics; thin yet strong enough, but delicate-looking like his mother. Not like a Chilton at all, not even in the things he cared about. Keith was no outdoor man and freely admitted it.

'Your uncle wanted you to be like him — or at least to care for the things he did,' Neville Shaw said. As the old man's friend and lawyer, he perhaps understood more what lay behind all this than anyone else was likely to.

'Yes, but to leave a Will like that!' Keith burst out, then turned back to the window. He had been very fond of his uncle, a strong, bluff, hearty outdoor type, and it was difficult to think, even now, that he was dead. 'He despised attention to sickness,' he said in a low tone. 'He loathed my laboratory — '

'But he let you set it up here,' Neville Shaw broke in quickly, 'and if you've been listening to me reading this document you will see that he isn't asking you to dismantle it all and go away somewhere else. You can leave it all here, continue working here — so long as you comply with the terms of the Will.'

Keith turned slowly round. 'Which is a contradiction in itself wouldn't you say?' He smiled wryly. 'You don't know the times my uncle interrupted me in my laboratory and the library, trying by every ruse he knew, to get me out of these, and out of doors with him.'

'He told me time and time again that it wasn't good for you to be in there,' Neville said quickly. 'He honestly believed you'd be better out riding with him, making plans for the improvement of the estate. It's a big estate. It needs someone constantly to keep watch over it, you realise that?'

'I only realise one thing,' Keith said. 'I'm a scientist, not a countryman. My uncle wanted to change me. And he's used this Will of his to do so now, what he couldn't do when he was alive. He just couldn't see,' he said, banging the table with a frustrated fist, 'that my life, my whole life, is dedicated to finding the answer to the bug that took my aunt off, out there in the Tropics. There's nothing much else that interests me.'

'Except writing that medical book on your pet bug,' the solicitor sighed. 'Your uncle told me. You're no longer connected with the life in hospital. Can't you leave the research to the research wallahs, my boy, and get out more, please your uncle this way?'

'Get out more and meet the person he wanted me to marry. Oh, yes, I suppose there is such a person existing. There must be, because he knew very well I didn't know any young woman who'd want to marry me!' and he hunched his shoulders and turned away again.

The solicitor packed up his papers. They were the last in the big room, after the reading of the Will. It had been a lengthy document, its bequests remembering servants and old friends, people the late Edward Chilton had known in his vigorous outdoor life, people who had been shocked and surprised at his dying so suddenly. That his heart should have been shaky had not occurred to any of them. And now, there was this tall young man with the thin sensitive face and dark hair, the earnest brown eyes under straight uncompromising black brows, and the surprisingly firm mouth and chin — the

4

last of the Chiltons and as confirmed a bachelor as the old man had dreaded.

'Your uncle did mention Melanie Radlett,' Neville said, with a half smile. 'Well, why not? Her passion is horses. She's a good judge of horseflesh. She'd fill the stables here again. Chilton Grange was famous for its bloodstock once. And she's very keen and knowledgeable on running the outside of the estate, she — '

' — rides to hounds,' Keith broke in. 'And she's vigorous like my uncle, and she talks forcefully. She does everything forcefully. And that is the person my uncle wanted for my wife, and made it impossible for me to inherit unless that was so?'

'Well, now, let's not get overheated,' Neville broke in quickly. 'It isn't quite as tied up as that. It doesn't have to be Melanie,' and he half smiled as Keith turned round hopefully. 'I mean your uncle (if you had been listening hard enough to what I was reading so carefully to you not long ago) didn't tie you down to any particular young woman. Only to a type of young woman.'

'The outdoor type,' Keith snapped.

'Well, yes, I suppose that was in his mind,' the solicitor said slowly. 'The thing is, he wanted you to marry. He wanted someone to care about you as he did. He wanted heirs. Now don't look so horrified — this is a big house and I'm quite sure that your laboratory could be kept far enough out of earshot of the nursery. The thing is, Keith, your uncle merely *said* in effect that you were to marry someone who wasn't (and I quote again) involved with laboratories and books.'

'Which just about removes the unfortunate young woman from everything that interests me,' Keith said bitterly.

'Oh, I don't know. Would you be prepared to consider marriage in order to inherit, if you could find someone compatible? I mean, you do care for the Grange, I believe?'

Keith thought about it. 'I don't know. I only know that I'd hate to have to take my laboratory to pieces and move it elsewhere or in fact find a place for it elsewhere, as quiet and suitable in every way as the corner of this house that I occupy. How could I continue to write the book on my findings without his excellent library here? I shudder to think of being uprooted. All my work here, my data, my — well, the atmosphere, everything!'

'Well, there you are — !'

'Well, there you are!' Keith echoed angrily. 'But all that would go, even if I did marry, because a wife means a social existence, and there would be people and parties and other people's children and animals, and horses and — ' He shrugged angrily.

The solicitor sighed. 'I know how you feel. Think it over. You can go on living here, as you know, for six months, but if you haven't married — or at least made firm arrangements to — by then, I'm afraid you lose the Grange.'

'Tell me again: who does it go to?' Keith asked, thinking.

'Now don't think you can come to terms with someone else owning it, to keep your laboratory here, because that's not on,' the solicitor warned. 'No, the place will go to — '

'Oh, I remember, I remember! That society to do with advanced treating of the soil and novelty farming,' Keith broke in angrily. 'No, of course I couldn't stay here. Oh, well, I suppose I'll have to think of someone to approach to propose marriage to. *I can't*. It's not right! One shouldn't go into marriage that way!' he said, half to himself.

'Why not meet a lot of young women, until you find one you like for herself?' the solicitor softly suggested.

'Such as who, and where?' Keith retorted. 'I only know a few women in other laboratories and they're my rivals, and not — well, not the sort my uncle had in mind. No, they don't have to be connected with my sort of life at all, I recall. That was clever of him! Or was it your idea?'

'Not mine,' the solicitor repudiated hastily. 'All your uncle's, I assure you. Now I tell you what. You've been through a pretty rotten time this last week. Now it's time to relax. You do like history, I believe?'

'I read history for pleasure. What about it?'

'Only that my nephew is seeing a Marlow play tonight. I don't know whether you'd care for it. But it *is* in London, and you could dine with his party afterwards. Give it a try, even if you hate it. You can always walk out on them,' and he looked so appealing and helpful that Keith said, laughing, 'Oh, very well! You're a trier! But I warn you, I won't come away from there tonight, engaged to be married! I don't suppose my uncle included the stage either, did he?'

'That's an odd thing about the Will,' the solicitor frowned. 'He doesn't rule it out. He only says 'someone not

9

connected with any of the things
remotely concerning laboratories and
books'.'

★　★　★

Chilton Grange was in such deep
country that the sudden visit to London
night life was in the nature of a shock to
Keith, who had not been to any town in
the evening for some months. The
solicitor had been very kind and
helpful, arranging with his nephew for
this evening, and the nephew was a
decent sort of fellow, Keith thought.
But neither of them had any idea of
how Keith winced at the brightness of
the lights, and the noises everywhere.
He tried, to take his mind off his
discomfort, to analyse the cacophony of
sounds. He thought he hated the street
noises most, particularly when the taxi
from the station was caught in one of
the many traffic jams. Then, too, he had
forgotten that London was now a
multi-racial city. It had a cosmopolitan

10

air about it that didn't appeal to him at all. He loathed neon signs and advertisements, he loathed the kind of window-dressing he saw around him, and the slow-moving noisy masses of people, all talking at once. Glimpses of restaurants in the narrow side streets, huge advertisements peeling from hoardings and walls, the stills outside the cinemas, all displeased him, and the rain that made the reflections of all the lights doubly brighter, more glaring, particularly disturbed him. Sharp needles of rain pointed down; a cold rain.

Simon Turnbull, Neville's nephew, was perhaps the best kind of person to take Keith in charge that evening. He was a cheerful young man and didn't really understand why anyone should hate London, but his uncle had briefed him well, and this was an important client. Like most of his uncle's clients, rather eccentric, too, but Simon had a healthy respect for big money, and used his considerable skills to find a suitable place to eat, one that would soothe Keith's frayed nerves, and someone equally suitable to make a fourth. His fiancée, Joan Oram, suggested Verena West, which didn't help.

'Don't be silly, love,' he begged her. 'Bad enough that we couldn't get tickets for that dreary historical play he wanted to see, but to include the star of the show we *are* springing on him — !'

Joan said, smiling broadly, 'Verena's always insisting she can act so now's her chance. She's supposed to know about the country, too. She can talk about that, as well.'

'Okay, Verena it is, though I don't think it's a good idea.'

'We might have two more, to help out. I suggest Mummy's new doctor and his wife. They can talk 'shop' if all else fails.'

Dr. Thorn was an inspiration. He was so much like the elderly people Keith's uncle had invited to play cards with him, that Keith eased out and after chatting with the Thorns, he almost accepted the flamboyant Verena in his stride.

She said, on meeting him, 'London chokes me. I sometimes think I shall die if I can't get back to the countryside, somehow.' In her elegant dark dress and discreet jewellery, she was reassuring enough for Keith, who didn't know it was the clothes she wore for her part as the lady of the manor.

She said it so sincerely that she caught Keith's interest. 'Which part of the country did you come from?' he wanted to know.

Verena never left herself without a way out. 'My dear, from all over the place. My parents were on the stage, but while they played the towns, they had me brought up in the nearby countryside. Best for a child. I have lovely memories.'

'What made you go on the stage in London yourself, then?' he asked, in a puzzled voice.

'My dear, what else could I do? I was conditioned for acting, because of my parents. When they died, I had to kick for myself. I don't mind telling you, I don't like the life. I would give everything I possessed to be proposed to by some country gentleman and never have to see London again. Well, not often, that is.'

Joan, taking on the Thorns to allow Verena and Keith the opportunity to get acquainted, wondered how Verena was going to get out of that one, if Keith proposed to her. But Verena was equal to it.

'But I don't suppose a country gentleman would ever see me as his wife,' Verena said sadly. 'You've just acquired a country house, I believe. What made you leave it to come to London?' and she drew him out to talk about the Grange. But Joan was amused to discover that what Keith was telling Verena wasn't personal stuff, but what anyone could find out from a visit to the village or a talk with any of the local tradespeople. Keith was a close one. She wondered if it were worth taking a bet with her incorrigible Simon, that Verena wouldn't catch Keith Chilton.

But at least Keith didn't seem so uneasy when they arrived at the theatre; not even when he realised what sort of show he was being asked to see. He silently sat through it, and Joan couldn't even estimate whether he was very much interested in Verena on stage, any more than he had been before.

'He tackles everything — even watching a show — as if it was a duty or an exam or something,' she complained to her fiancé.

Simon chuckled. 'Well, I like him, in spite of my uncle's dilemma. I've got the odd idea the chap is sound, the sort of person who'd take on a burden, not side-step it. I say, I hope he doesn't choose Verena to marry.'

'Well, what are we working so hard for?' Joan demanded.

'Uncle said try everything,' Simon explained.

'Then we'd better take him back-stage. It will be experience,' Joan chuckled. 'I bet he's never been backstage in his life.'

They were at the bar at the time. Keith had gone outside to stretch his legs. He didn't smoke or drink, it seemed. Simon, who found this discon-certing, was quite sure the idea of a backstage visit would put him off Verena. 'Better not,' he said quickly. 'You'd never get him there. You must see what he's like! My uncle will kill me if I upset him.'

Yet when it came to suggesting it after the show, Keith said unexpectedly that he would like to go, and meet everyone.

They thought this was his bashful way of saying 'Verena' and exchanged glances, but Keith really meant it and he was particularly thinking about the elderly woman who had had a walking-on part. He thought she might well have really been elderly. She walked like that, and her grey hair didn't look like a wig.

She was someone's secretary in the play, and all she had to do was to walk on with some papers, put them in a file on the desk and walk out, but she got a round of applause for it. He had the odd but driving desire to meet someone who didn't even manage to get a line to say, but who had stopped the show even though the leading lady was on stage.

It was not a good moment for their visit. Verena had just had a row with her producer about that walking-on part. 'She stopped the show — when *I* was on!' she complained, before someone popped their head kindly round the door and advised, 'Bellow some other time, darling — visitors ahoy!' and the producer patted her shoulder and said, 'What do you care, love? You're the star — she didn't even have a line.'

Verena said darkly, 'She'd better not have,' and gave her attention to dressing. 'Keep those visitors at bay till I'm ready,' she warned him. 'One is going to be madly rich if he inherits from his old uncle. I want him.'

The producer grinned. 'What about poor old Seton? Wasn't he rich enough for you? He's out front as usual.'

Verena looked up. Seton, with his monocle on its black band, the impediment in his speech, and his doting eyes following her, were not what she wanted to remember at this moment. 'The operative word being 'old',' she snapped. 'This one's young. And besides, I'm going off Seton Nolan.'

She finished in double quick time and came dramatically out, sure of her audience behind the scenes. 'Darlings!' She put out both arms to embrace Simon and his fiancée, the Thorns, Keith, all at once. 'We must *do* something special tonight! Here's poor Keith bogged down in the respectable atmosphere of the Criterion Hotel and I bet he hasn't seen anything in London worth seeing! We must take him around tonight.'

'No, I have to get up early!' Keith protested. Verena was no longer like the woman he had dined with, talking of country matters and pining to get away from London. She had forgotten to preserve that image and he noticed and was wary.

'What for darling?' she demanded.

'I have to find a secretary,' he said, unwillingly.

'Well, darling, let your solicitor find you one! What's a solicitor for? Tell your uncle, Simon!' and she took Keith's arm and bore him away, Simon, Joan, the Thorns and the leading man behind her, amiably wrangling about who should ride in which car.

Keith looked round for the grey-haired extra, but there were too many people churning around and he didn't suppose he'd be allowed to speak to her, anyway.

And then, quite unexpectedly, he caught sight of her, standing half way up the stairs, her glasses slightly askew, looking reflectively at him. He had the urge to go back, but he was being swept along with the crowd.

The cold night air at the stage door, hit them. A knot of people pressed forward, with little books and pencils. Autograph hunters. This was Keith's first experience of being crushed in an eager, determined crowd. He glanced at Verena, and saw that she and her leading man were busily signing, and loving it. Keith asked himself what he had expected.

'Quite a good crowd tonight,' Verena said with satisfaction, when they were packed in the cars and crawling away from the theatre to the first night spot they had decided on. She was pleased, he saw.

'You'd miss all that, if you went back to the country,' he reminded her.

She looked at Keith reflectively. 'No, darling, you don't understand me at all, do you? Wherever I am, whatever I happen to be doing, I get involved. That's me! I like people, and what makes them tick. But you have to be with them, all the way. No good looking all stiff, darling — they won't let you in, if you do!'

Keith was astonished. That was what his uncle had always said, though the wording might have been different.

All the same, he wasn't convinced. While Verena was talking, he was thinking that he had only to endure one night at the hotel chosen by his solicitor, then tomorrow he would gladly return to Grinton Heath. Just a few hours of getting through traffic, the press of town people enjoying themselves; a few more hours of noise and cigarette smoke and the odour of rich food and wine. And then ... he thought nostalgically of the smell of the land round the Grange, through the open window, just before dawn broke. The first cheep of a bird, the first disgruntled sounds of a tractor being coaxed into action, the first voice — and he recalled how sweetly voices carried in the clean country air.

'What did you think of the place?'

Verena demanded, as they left the first night spot.

'It had blue lighting,' Keith managed, with distaste.

The others were amused. 'Of course, darling! It was called The Blue Dream!' and they all kept laughing.

The second night spot had more conventional lighting but a great deal more noise. Keith would have given a lot to have had the courage to break out of the party and go back to his hotel but the Thorns, who were middle-aged, were sticking it out stoically.

But tomorrow, tomorrow, he would be back at work in his lab and again tackling the problem that gave him no rest. He thought of his aunt's face, when he first heard that the disease had gone too far, and that they could do no more for her than they could for the children he had been seeing the day before, at the nearby hospital. The urgency of the problem even blotted out the noise and brightness of London at night.

It was Verena's voice, talking to the others, that brought him back. He had missed some of the conversation. 'Candy is much better in the part of the old secretary,' he heard Verena say. 'What made the audience react like that? Did she trip or something?'

Nobody else wanted to answer that, it was clear, so Keith said, 'Oh, was that little part only for tonight? What will she do tomorrow, then?' and they all looked at him, surprised that he should be interested.

Verena shrugged. 'She'll be 'resting' again. They usually wash dishes in the hotels, but that one nips round the corner to the Ace Bureau. She was a typist or something, before she tried for the stage. She should have stayed that way,' she finished, and then, at a glance from Joan, Verena added quickly, 'Well, what I mean is, it's no way to earn your living at her time of life. She really *is* an oldie. Well, quite forty, and getting nowhere fast. I'm sorry for the bit parts, I really am. I was only saying to my producer tonight . . . '

Keith didn't bother to listen. He memorised the Ace Agency and wondered why. There was no sense in wanting to see that person again but he did.

Perhaps he was like the audience tonight. They had liked her. No reason — she hadn't spoken or even looked beyond the footlights. In the part, she had had to be intensely interested in those papers she was replacing, and she had been just that. Intensely interested in what she had been doing.

I want a secretary, Keith told himself unexpectedly. Someone to arrange things. Someone to rely on, and to talk to. To understand the need to get on with the work of tracing that bug. To understand that no social existence, no person, nothing, was so important as that. The work. Someone, moreover, to work on my book with me, he told himself, remembering that mounting untidy sheaf of precious handwritten notes that he lived in terror of either losing, or getting out of sequence.

He went to the private party with the others and stuck it out. It was always his policy to do nothing to attract adverse attention. To want to go home to bed now, would do just that. So, almost sleeping on his feet, and bored to tears, he waited for the others to make a move to go home, while his hostess poured out her domestic troubles in his ear.

People drank and talked and laughed, and music blared but no one listened. How, he asked himself, as they at last decided to depart, how was he going to cope with a wife and parties like this when all he craved for was quiet, to think and to work. Quiet, to enjoy, in the very limited spare time he allowed himself, books and good music.

The next day he presented himself at the Ace Bureau. A neat office with a smart middle-aged woman with a brisk manner, sitting behind a desk. She seemed to have a lot of pretty young typists who were equally fitted for the social life after hours, and when she heard what Keith's special requirements were, she was quite sure she had nothing to suit him, and recommended him to other agencies.

He trudged round them all, and even described that grey-haired woman, in the hope that she might have been in, but he had forgotten to ask her name, and it probably wasn't the same as her stage name.

Hopeless, he went back to his hotel for lunch. He had an odd sense of loss. He was tired of London. He would have to battle alone, think of something. Perhaps in the end it would be better to let the house go: find somewhere to set up his laboratory, with a desk and a typewriter, and to creep away before Melanie Radlett could persuade him that life would be very good with her, her father and limitless well-stocked stables. She haunted him while he ate, and when he escaped to his hotel room afterwards, he asked himself why he was allowing himself to be pushed into this situation. But he knew the answer: his uncle's wishes.

The telephone jangled. He was half inclined not to answer it. He was, at the time, flinging things busily into his overnight bag. But his hospital days and old habits forced him to pick up the receiver. A quiet well-bred voice was put through to him.

'I understand you need a secretary,' it said.

For no reason at all, he was excited. He hadn't heard the voice before, yet he felt it was important to him. 'You're from the Ace Bureau?' he guessed. They had found someone!

'No, I was at the theatre last night. Backstage I heard you say as you were leaving, that you wanted to engage a secretary. I had a walking on part but I *am* a secretary.'

It was *her*, he told himself, and he wondered why he was so excited. She was much older than he was, and he didn't even know what her work was like. But there it was; he was as excited as some men get when they meet a pretty alluring young girl.

It sounded in his ears, that wild excitement, as he burst out, 'But I've been out all morning round the Agencies, looking for you! How did you find me?'

'I heard Verena say where you were staying,' the voice said calmly, adding, 'My name is Rachel Beamish.'

2

Neville Shaw had been warned by the old man, before he died, that Keith was unpredictable, but he hadn't expected this result to his own suggestion that Keith should go to London.

'What's wrong with my finding a secretary for myself?' Keith exploded, when the solicitor protested. 'I'm best equipped to know what I want. She suits me, and in the week she's been working for me, I've been more comfortable than my poor old uncle was with the staff he managed to get.'

'But it seems you know nothing about her! What's her background? How old is she? What about references?'

'I don't know any of those things and I don't care. I only know that she's so good at her work that I don't have to tell her a thing. She almost reads my mind.'

That didn't please Neville at all. 'What happened that evening you went to the theatre with Simon and his party? I thought you'd . . . well, find that Verena was rather nice. Simon said — '

Keith looked rather grim. 'I didn't know it was your idea to try and matchmake in that quarter! I thought it was all on the part of your nephew,' and he added, in a displeased voice, 'And it wasn't a Marlowe play, either. Still, I have to be grateful to you all, I suppose, for arranging that evening, because I did meet my secretary through it,' he added, trying to be fair, though he wouldn't explain any further what he meant by that.

'Well, let's see what's so special about her,' Neville said tartly, 'while we go through these investments, because I didn't bring my own secretary with me.'

'You'll be delighted with Rachel,' Keith said.

Neville picked up his briefcase and glanced quickly at his new client. On

Christian name terms already, and a shy person like the old man's nephew. Glumly he thought, she's heard of the money. Or how else could Keith have been suited so quickly?

'I rather thought you'd look for a wife first, so we could settle the estate. Then you could go back to your research.'

Keith scowled fiercely as he led the way to the library. 'If you're tilting at Melanie Radlett, it's no go. She's horse mad.'

'Melanie Radlett's all right,' Neville said quickly. 'I've told you — your uncle liked her!'

'Well, I don't,' Keith said definitely. 'Then there's a girl called Carol Harris, who keeps an art shop in Bexfield. She stopped me in Bexfield High Street and insisted that my uncle had ordered some perfectly hideous wooden candlesticks — '

Neville snorted with laughter. 'A good try, but no, I think not. Still, you should be careful in that quarter,' he warned. 'Her grandmother was a very close friend of your uncle's. She'll expect to come over. Besides, Carol's not a bad sort of girl.'

'I didn't say she was,' Keith said quietly, stopping to look out across a view that never failed to enchant him. 'I am afraid I shall have to be able to *like* the girl I ask to marry me.'

Neville sighed. 'Well, what about Hazel Masters? Foxmile Farm. Going to be a vet. Farming family. You'd never have to worry about the estate, with that lot. You must have met her — '

'No, I never did,' Keith said firmly. 'In my uncle's time I kept out of the way of the lot of them. Rachel keeps them away from me now. I don't know what I'd do without her.'

'Well, let's see this paragon you seem to have found for yourself,' Neville growled, as they arrived at the library door.

Rachel's neatly styled grey head was bent over a paperstrewn table in one of the windows. She politely rose to her feet as the men entered, and Neville, who had his share of modern young stenographers, thought nostalgically that here was the last bastion of respectful manner to the boss.

She was a paragon, too, he discovered. He had to admit it, after she had taken down a very long list of fast-dictated notes and figures, and calmly gave him her notebook to read back.

'I don't read shorthand, madam,' he said coldly, and he couldn't help himself staring at her. In spite of her efficiency and her correctness, there was something not quite right. She bothered him. That face was too smooth and unlined for an elderly spinster shorthand typist, but the hands were square and made for working, a thing which he approved of. He didn't care for long soft white fingers colour-tipped. This Rachel had nothing like that. And she was so sensible. He tried to shake off his unease, and told himself, as the men sat back to enjoy a smoke while Rachel typed the notes, that Keith had, perhaps with sheer luck, done very well for himself.

Rachel didn't smoke. She retired to the end of the room where a small desk was fixed up with a portable typewriter, an adjustable lamp, and a swivelling fitment of trays to keep her papers tidy. A sensible little person in a pleated tweed skirt and a no-nonsense blouse and cardigan. Neat but hardly smart, and really no fortune-hunter. Just a comfortable woman to work with, protect a chap from intruders and any other worries.

'All the same,' the solicitor told Keith, as the two men walked down the steps of the mansion and stood taking the air on this very pleasant day, 'you will have to stop your hiding from life. You'll have to manage the estate — '

'No need. I know nothing of country affairs. Rachel does that. She's first rate. The men get on well with her, too.'

'That's all very well, but — '

'And another thing,' Keith broke in

firmly, 'she rather likes an all-male staff in the house, which appeals to me. I'm fed up with the silly housemaids that were always coming and going, in my uncle's time. The men keep the place clean. Rachel gets chaps out of the Navy. They're first rate.'

'I don't like it,' Neville said suspiciously. 'Such efficiency and consenting to work in an off-the-beaten-track location like this. Now, if she were young, I'd begin to think — but no. How old would you think she is?'

'I don't know,' Keith repeated, coldly. 'I'm not interested. I like her for herself. Her age doesn't matter.'

Neville glanced sharply at him. The old man had had fears about how Keith would react to all this. Just how eccentric could a young man be? He seemed to like this older woman too much.

'Well, never mind that. I forgot to mention the June the First Ball,' he told Keith, in some exasperation.

Keith was surprised and indignant.

'I'm not having that — I haven't the time!'

'I do really think,' the solicitor said mildly, 'that I must send you another copy of the will. You must have surely lost yours. Or perhaps you haven't had time to read it. The social dates in your late uncle's calendar have to be kept. That's one of them.'

Keith stared. 'And are you saying that if I get fed up and throw in the towel, and this house goes to the farming research lot, that they're going to keep up the social calendar?'

'Of course not,' the solicitor said impatiently. 'Different thing altogether. They're not family. You are. Everyone expects it. Besides, your uncle wanted you to marry, and keeping the social calendar will help you meet suitable young women. I don't have to explain all this to you, surely!'

Keith gave it thought. 'No, you don't,' he agreed at last.

'You won't have to do a thing yourself. I'll even find you a hostess, if you like. Simon's fiancée would, I daresay.'

Keith said, 'You've got it all worked out, haven't you? I daresay you were behind the whole bright idea of this Will.'

'No, I could never have thought up such a plan,' Neville said modestly, as he took his leave. 'It was all your uncle's doing.'

Rachel looked thoughtfully at Keith as he returned to the library. 'I have the feeling that your solicitor doesn't like me,' she remarked.

'Probably because he hasn't a secretary like you,' Keith said shortly. 'Or because I didn't ask him to find a secretary for me. Never mind him. There's something else I want to talk to you about. I don't like being forced into marriage, but I am and there it is. I have to agree that it's sensible to get it over with, so I can forget it and settle down to work. Now, my solicitor tells me my uncle rather had Melanie Radlett in mind.'

There was no constraint between them. All his shyness vanished when he talked to Rachel. He didn't even look at her as he continued, 'Now what, in the opinion of a sensible person like you — *what* would you think of that redheaded rider to hounds?'

He was glaring moodily out of the window, but at the continued silence, he brought his glance back to Rachel. Her eyebrows were raised so high that he could see them over the top of her dark-rimmed glasses.

'What offends you most?' she asked icily. 'The colour of her hair or the fact that she hunts?'

He stared, then he laughed. He had an attractive laugh; low, explosive, infectious. 'That's right, you pull me up if I'm ungallant to the ladies. That's me. Well, I'm not enamoured of the hard-riding ones, of course. I don't like horses, personally.'

'Red hair, then?'

'It was ill-mannered of me,' he

allowed. 'But I don't like redheads,' he admitted.

'On principle? Because of what you've heard of them?' she probed. 'Or for some other reason? If it's personal, you'd better brief me, so I don't make a gaffe.'

He looked into her eyes, his pipe poised in his hand. There *was* something about Rachel. He liked her so much. It was the cosy sort of comradeship that he had always instinctively felt should be between married people. And it would be missing in this marriage he was being forced to make.

'I think it's because of always having had thrust at me the name of a particular redhead,' he said at last. 'The daughter of a cousin's wife. No relation at all, really, but whenever that girl's mother appears, she always wants to tell me how wonderful this redhead daughter of hers is. I hate having someone's virtues thrust at me. Lydia Lawrence,' he finished bitterly.

'But you've never met her?'

'Heavens, no, and I don't want to. I almost did, though, as it happens. They tell me she went to my old hospital to train as a nurse, so I shifted. If she or her mother comes here, keep them away at all costs! Understood?'

'Understood,' Rachel said, in a queer voice.

'Why do you say it like that?'

'I don't know,' she mused. 'I suppose it's because up till now you struck me as being such a . . . such a *good* young man. Old-fashioned term, that, but it's all I can think of. I wouldn't have thought you would be prejudiced, especially about someone you've never even met. She might be all right, that girl.'

'No, she couldn't be. Not from what I've heard of her.' He bit hard on his pipe. 'Besides, she — the whole of her family, in fact — destroy one's peace of mind. I've only had experience of her mother. My cousin Amelia has thought of one thing and one thing only, for years. That's my uncle's money.'

'How can you be sure of that?' she asked angrily.

'It isn't your problem, except to keep them away from me,' he told her. 'But you must know, to understand what's required of you. My uncle had a round-up of his relatives a few years ago. Seeing where they were, what their circumstances were, whether he could bring himself to like any of them, I suppose.' He chuckled at the thought. 'You'd have liked the old boy, Rachel. An out-and-out countryman, blunt to the point of embarrassment, but the soul of honesty and a heart of gold. He set his solicitor to find all the relatives, and discovered me.'

Rachel had other ideas about a man who couldn't give generously but had to make these worrying conditions for a person like Keith who had a worthwhile job he was anxious to get on with. She said, 'Where were you? At home?'

Keith got up and went to his favourite window. Shimmering mist touched the growing things so that they sparkled like jewels. Just one aspect in the changing kaleidoscope of views from this window, where his uncle had loved to stand. 'No, I had no home,' he said. 'I'd got through university somehow. I only wanted to qualify and then to go into research. A hand-to-mouth existence. He made me come here to live.'

'He forced you?' She couldn't believe it.

'A man as rich as he was, *can* force people. He somehow persuaded my landlord to turn me out, so I was glad to come here for the sake of somewhere to bring all my precious equipment I'd laboriously saved up for. It was a dirty trick.'

She stared up at him. He shook his head at her. 'You know, Rachel, you sometimes have the same look on your face that my uncle had, when I was being sorry for myself.' He laughed. 'Oh, well, I suppose from my Cousin Amelia's vantage point, it looked as if I had worked my way in, especially as my uncle got interested and insisted on financing a super laboratory for me.'

'Which hospital were you at?' she asked. He told her.

'What are you looking like that for? Did you know someone there?' he asked sharply, but she merely shrugged. 'It's hard to think of you in a white coat,' she said.

The awkward moment passed. 'Go on,' she invited.

'Well, then,' he continued, turning away with that quiet anger of his, 'to force me, in that will, to *marry* in order to inherit, to keep that fine lab he'd fitted up for me ! That really infuriated me.' He almost added that it had hurt him, too, but that would have been to go too far in the tearing down of barriers.

'He sounds as if he meant well,' Rachel observed mildly. 'He probably felt you'd be more comfortable, married. After all, it was *his* money, *his* house. Surely he could have a little fun in dispensing it all at his departure?'

He turned sharply and looked at her, surprising a half smile which she quickly dampened.

He came over to her and stood looking down at her. 'Oh, *you*!' he said, laughing softly. 'Do you know what I wish?'

'No. What?'

He was appalled at what he had been nearly going to say. He had been going to say that they had found the perfect companionship, and that he would consider his troubles over if he could marry *her* in order to inherit. *Rachel*. His grey-haired secretary. The person, his thoughts raced on, who at times was as young in outlook, in manner of speaking, as he was himself.

He flushed to the roots of his hair and turned away, but as she insisted on hearing what it was he had to say, he improvised.

'I was just thinking how well we get on together; how comfortable and smooth you make everything for me. I suppose I'm afraid of losing you.'

'You might want me to go one day,' she said severely.

'Heavens, why would I want to do that? After a week's experience of your particular kind of shielding, I'd be terrified to lose you now!'

'Oh, is that all you want me for — to shield you? To type your notes? To listen to you? Come now, Mr. Chilton, there are plenty of good secretaries, some a lot younger than I am!'

'*Keith*,' he corrected her. 'And no other secretary would be quite like you,' he murmured, staring at her. 'You've got a special quality. Sometimes you seem old enough for me to unload all my secret thoughts on to you. And there are times when you seem so young — my age in fact — and I'm quite sure we could go out on the spree together and have a thumping good time!'

'Spree? With my employer?' she said indignantly, which made him snort with laughter.

'That's another thing. My uncle

complained that I had no laughter in me, but consider the times you've made me laugh since you've been here!' And before she could answer that, he strode out of the room, his head in the clouds over something he had just thought of. The typical scientist, she thought, shaking her head. He had already forgotten he had said all those things, which was perhaps as well.

She sat staring at the various piles of notes she had around her. What was she going to do? She must find someone for him to marry, someone who wouldn't disturb him. He must have his peace of mind. In her heart she didn't think he would be successful in finding this cure, whatever it was, and she felt from what the solicitor had said, that his uncle hadn't, either. That was the impression she'd got. But a man must have something to do, and anything that kept him as absorbed and happy as that laboratory was, she was sure, a good thing, if he had no ambitions other than that. Keith didn't want to ride to hounds. He was no ladies' man. The Stock Exchange clearly didn't appeal to him. What else would he do? Go back to hospital? And what woman would want to marry him and be content to leave it at that? What woman, came the disquieting further thought, would want to marry him, and leave him to the cosy companionship of Rachel herself, who must work with him on his book?

Later that day the Colonel came over, with all the assurance of an old neighbour and friend. A tall, militarylooking man with a fierce way of glaring at the staff, through a monocle. 'Go and tell your chief I want to see him — matter of life and death. Now don't waste time, my good woman — go and tell him!'

Rachel wasn't intimidated. 'I'm here, sir,' she said softly, standing behind her desk with quiet dignity, 'to keep from him all his friends who have matters of such importance to impart to him. I do assure you!'

The Colonel looked at her suspiciously, and surprised a twinkle in her eyes. 'Damn me,' he said, 'he's picked himself a fine secretary; can I tempt you to come and work for me, heh? Could do with someone who stands her ground. Now be a dear, and go and tell him this is a matter of horseflesh. He'll be roaring mad if he lets this chance go! What are you shaking your head for, woman?'

'He'll never get roaring mad, sir, about anything, but he'll be very upset if I disturb him in the laboratory, so shall I call you up later, at dinner time, say?'

'What, disturb a chap at his evening meal?'

'Mr. Chilton would rather be disturbed at table than in his lab,' she said politely, but with such finality, that the Colonel hesitated and was lost.

'Well, I tell you what! I'll leave a note for him. Perhaps he'd consent to meet me at my place and see this filly. He really mustn't let up a chance like this.'

He looked sharply at her. 'Know anything about horses, by the way?'

He didn't expect anything but a negative. Rachel surprised him.

'Well, yes, sir, my father — but don't ever let Mr. Chilton know, will you? My knowledge of horseflesh is one of my assets I kept from him because I wanted this country job so badly.'

The Colonel prided himself on never being swayed by someone's personality but Rachel's was deceptive, insidious. He said, 'Damn me, woman, what's your name? Rachel, is it? Have you got a minute? Well, later, then. Got a car, have you? Well, you should have! Like to show you over my stables, if you'd care for it.'

'I'd like that very much, sir,' Rachel said firmly. Horses . . . so that was the way the father of Melanie was going to work, she thought, as she rang for him to be shown out.

Phelps came back, and coughed discreetly, before unloading a few more of his useful reminiscences on her. This prince of butlers was one of the oldest of the late Mr. Chilton's staff.

'If I may say so, miss, the late master never took any advice given by Colonel Radlett. He had too many — ah — how shall I put it?'

Rachel, remembering her own father and his stable talk, supplied exactly the verbal description that Phelps was dancing nervously round. Phelps looked at her in shocked respect.

Rachel dealt kindly with him. 'As I told the Colonel, I didn't let Mr. Keith know how much I knew about horse-flesh. It's not part of my duties here, after all,' she finished delicately.

'No, miss, as you say, miss,' Phelps said, with another cough, but she knew she had won an extensive victory there, and made a very useful ally. 'If I may suggest, miss, Mr. Keith hasn't been out of the house for almost a fortnight. Needs fresh air. Perhaps you might think of something important enough to take him to, say, Melmerstead on market day. A very interesting place, that. Or even to the coast, not much further on. Not looking himself, Mr. Keith. His uncle used to worry.'

Rachel promised she would, and thought about it. The next day was the day, according to Phelps, that Melanie Radlett rode over, to 'just drop by'. Rachel gathered that Phelps, unlike his late master, didn't care much for Melanie.

Keith emerged for lunch with no great interest. It would be served, he knew, at the long dining table in the Gold Room, facing north. It had seemed a cold, lonely place in his uncle's time, each of them absurdly seated at each end of it. The interminable parties of his uncle's, with all his male friends and their uninteresting wives seated round that long table, had seemed colder, lonelier gatherings. He wondered if he dared ask for a small round table to be set up in the lilac and rose room behind the library. The Lady's Parlour of Regency days, where, as pictured in the tapestries on the walls, the ladies had sat at their tambour frames, stitching and talking. A nice room to sit in with Rachel.

He went and found her. 'I know you've stepped into the late housekeeper's shoes,' he said, 'but do you have to eat on a tray in her room, and leave me all alone in that cold dining room?'

'It wouldn't do for me to eat with you,' she told him.

'Oh, don't worry about what the rest of the staff think! Well, if you're going to persist in worrying, then let's go out!'

Rachel considered the point. Phelps had suggested it. Well, why not?

Keith mistook her silence. 'Oh, don't turn me down, Rachel. I've never asked a female to lunch before and I'll die of embarrassment if you refuse.'

'And if I accept after that, you'll never know if I did because of saving you embarrassment or fear of losing my job,' she retorted, then almost at once she smiled broadly and said, 'I'd love it, actually!'

He wanted so badly to take her in the big car the chaffeur had always driven his uncle about in, but Rachel promptly said no.

'We're not dressed for it! You in that trench coat and old felt, and me in this tweed and a raincoat. Whatever next! No, let's take the Land-Rover, then on the way back you can drive me over the estate and show me everything, as you promised.'

He gave it some thought and a hunted look came into his face.

'I think — ' he began, and then paused, colouring a little, and looking in a bothered way at the tablecloth. 'You see,' he tried again, 'I don't know very much about the married state. I've always lived with spinster aunts or bachelor uncles, and it seems to me that the whole of marriage — even to taking a meal together — is an intensely personal business.'

'Well,' she said quickly, 'let's start

from there. Why don't you take each one of these young women you know, in turn, to a meal? And see which one you couldn't bear to eat with for the rest of your life,' and she smiled.

'And where do you go from there?' he asked glumly. He tried to picture Melanie sitting where Rachel was. Melanie wouldn't like this pub at all. He replaced her in his mind with Carol, and remembered hearing someone say that Carol Harris and her arty pals had drinking competitions. He recoiled from the thought.

He shrugged. 'Hazel Masters might be least terrifying, but . . . her family's by way of being on my borders. If I took her out and then washed my hands of her, it might be awkward.'

'Might you wash your hands of her? What's she like?'

'She's training to be a vet. She looks attractive, clean-scrubbed, healthy, but there's a look in her eyes which makes me feel she thinks my mind works slowly.'

'Well, that's rot, of course,' Rachel said bracingly.

'Yes, but I couldn't have a wife with that opinion,' he said. 'Nor could I have a wife who is rude to staff and everyone in fact who doesn't like horses as much as she does.'

He was thinking of Melanie Radlett, Rachel thought. 'Carol Harris?' she suggested, without much hope.

'I don't like her friends. Anyway, she always has paint on her overall and clay on her hands and — ' He broke off, shrugging.

Rachel said briskly, 'Well, you'll see me with ink or carbon smears before you're much older,' but he countered that swiftly by saying, 'Yes, I know, but the odd thing about it is I don't mind how you look. You're — sort of — '

'Don't say 'different', *please*,' she begged him. 'That's what is said to younger women, when the man is trying to shoot a line,' and that made him laugh very much.

'Well, we've disposed of the lot of

them,' he said, as he prepared to settle the bill.

'Oh, I don't know. Have we?' she objected.

He was suddenly serious. 'Those three were closest to my uncle by way of their families being friends. I couldn't choose any other local girl, after turning down one of them. You do see that?' And that was a point even the astute Rachel had overlooked.

On the other side of Foxmile Farm were dense woods, and beyond that, the Pond Cottages, which were on Chilton land. The land was hilly, the surface slippery with recent rain. Rachel undertook the driving, and Keith let her. The atmosphere between them was so easy, he felt he was losing nothing by conceding that she might manage the driving better than he would, and she did.

Behind the wheel she looked different. As he pointed out the boundaries of his uncle's land, and the artificial views that had been created to his uncle's design, he kept looking at Rachel. On foot she had seemed short, bristling with determination, an age to correspond with that grey hair and those clothes. Now she had tied a scarf round her head, and she seemed slender, younger. He found himself considering her protectively, as she handled the Land-Rover with considerable skill. But she was very much his senior, wasn't she, he took himself to task? But he couldn't keep the protective feeling out, especially when she deliberately drove up a slope known as Holkin Bottom, where the land rose, tree-lined, then fell away sharply in a stony gradient that was almost a precipice, down to the floor of the old quarry. He said sharply, 'Look out, Rachel! Are you sure you know what you're doing?' but she just quietly, calmly handled the wheel, and poised at the edge and looked down.

'It's a wonderful view,' she said softly. 'I don't wonder at you not wanting to lose the Grange.'

But when they reached the Pond Cottages, she wasn't so pleased.

Tumbledown cottages, half covered in creepers blotched with wild colour, the original old red tiled roofs sagging in a way to delight the local artists, crouched too near for comfort, to the edge of a picturesque pond. Children played near it.

Rachel said pithily, 'Scum on the water, damp walls, very little mortar left after the creepers have eaten into it. What sort of property do you call that?'

'My uncle looked after these people well enough,' Keith said defensively. 'He tried to move the tenants out to new buildings. Good pre-fabricated dwellings nearer the Grange. But they wouldn't go. What can you do with people like that?'

Rachel sat tight-lipped, looking at it from a distance. 'Who are they?' she asked at last.

'Labourers. For our home farm. They like living in these cottages. They've always been here. Well, I can't do anything about it until I inherit. You know that. And I can't inherit without — ' and the word 'marriage' was left hanging uneasily in the air.

It disturbed the peace between them. They got out of the Land-Rover and strolled over to the cottages. The children stopped playing in the mud at the water's edge and stood staring. The pond smelt unpleasant in the shimmering heat.

One of the cottage doors opened and Fred Abney's wife stood apathetically regarding the visitors, as she leaned against the door lintel. 'If you want Fred, he's down to beet field, sir.'

She looked a slattern. She hadn't always. Keith felt a wild unreasoning anger that he should have this poor scene to show to Rachel. It ought to have been a model farm, good planning, with brisk, interested workers in white coats, moving quickly about the machinery, looking keen, secure in the knowledge that modern bungalow homes were awaiting them at the end of the day.

He felt guilt for no particular reason. After all, he remembered his uncle always saying that these people were extremely awkward when it came to the question of changing their abode and he could only think they didn't want to be moved because they had always lived there.

It really was a disgrace, as cottages went. It wasn't even dry — the whole land was sodden around there. Rachel looked at the virulent green of the grass and Keith was thinking that he really ought to have it drained. But it really was a beauty spot.

'My uncle used to want you to move out,' he said to Mrs. Abney, mainly to prove something to Rachel.

Mrs. Abney looked frightened and said, 'No, oh, please, we don't want to move out. We've always been here. It's our place,' but there was something odd about it. As if she feared a removal.

Keith didn't like it at all and when

they went back he carried with him a memory of Rachel bending down to push back the hair of one of the children, tilting its face up to look at it. It was a cute, *gamin* little face, but Rachel was looking at the skin.

'What were you looking at that child's face like that for?' he demanded, when they returned to the Land-Rover.

'Like what?'

'Have you been a nurse or something?' he was driven to say. There had been that touch of professionalism about the way she had touched the child.

Rachel said casually, 'Oh, it was nothing. Just a scratch — nothing a good clean up wouldn't have put right, but I don't think the mother would have taken kindly to that suggestion. Her sort believes the kids are happier dirty. Think nothing of it.' But she looked affronted by something. Smothered anger, he thought.

'I'll do something about them when I inherit . . . if I ever do,' he said quickly.

61

She didn't answer. She drove away from the place and went out of the field gate where Foxmile Farm was sign-posted. 'I'll show you a real farm, a desperately well-run farm,' he said bitterly, and his tone made her feel wretched.

Foxmile Farm was the pride and joy of the Masters family. A long, low, white-painted group of buildings, spot-less, hygienic — the factory type farm prettied up to look like the old style farmhouse, Rachel thought, with dis-taste.

Keith would have taken her to the front door and formally introduced her to Mrs. Masters, but he had bad luck. Hazel saw him first, and waved to him. She was in one of the barns, bending down to one of the dogs. Keith took Rachel across and performed his introduction there first.

Hazel glanced at Rachel, said 'Hi!' and promptly ignored her, giving all her attention to Keith, talking while she finished bandaging the paw of a Collie with some skill. Even in her holland overall and high boots, Hazel looked terribly well-groomed, and her back turned to Rachel, shutting her out of the conversation.

Keith said, 'We've been to the Pond Cottages,' but Hazel obviously had no interest in them.

She said, 'Oh. When do you move in on your inheritance? Isn't it exciting? Everyone's talking about it,' and she got up and dusted herself down, firmly took Keith by the arm and walked him out of the barn, two paces ahead of Rachel. 'Come and see Mother — she wants to talk to you about the June the 1st Ball — you *are* having it, as usual, aren't you?' A happy-looking girl with a wide mobile mouth, very blue eyes wide-spaced under straight dark brows, and hair more honey coloured than blonde, tightly waving, strong and springy hair. Everything about her was strong and springy, and she left no doubt, as she walked and talked, that she had known Keith a long time and wasn't going to have the secretary cutting in on the social scene here.

Keith said, 'Everyone must know how I shall hate having these social events but my solicitor is pushing me into it.'

'Have you decided on the hostess?' Hazel asked, looking him boldly in the eyes. Rachel felt slightly sick. These local girls were worse than the ones in town! Keith would be putty in this girl's hands. She had almost decided to join them and answer for him, when he forestalled her.

Much to Rachel's surprise — and to the other girl's, too, it appeared — Keith said coolly, 'Well, my solicitor did rather suggest the fiancée of his nephew Simon, but it occurred to me that it might be rather nice to give the job to someone in my family who feels she's been rather pushed out. She's used to entertaining, anyway, so it won't come hard to her. My cousin Amelia.'

3

'What on earth did you do that for?' Rachel burst out, when, having been shown in boring detail all over this model property by the over-proud father of Hazel, they could decently escape to the Land-Rover. 'You said you wouldn't have your cousin near you!'

Keith had surprised himself. Normally nothing in the world would have made him allow his cousin Amelia in the house. Moreover he had told Rachel so. It had been purely a defensive gesture. Hazel wanted the job. So too, would Melanie and Carol. In fact, in the eyes of the district, whoever got that job would be the one of his choice. He knew that. He had a hunted feeling. It was between those three girls, and he hoped he wouldn't have to see either of them again. But that was wishful thinking.

His agony of mind showed. Rachel watched him thoughtfully. It had given her a bad moment, too, when he had verbally committed himself in that way.

Rachel's puzzled silence bothered Keith. 'Look, I'm sorry I said that, after telling you so firmly to keep cousin Amelia out. Oh, dash, I'm sorry Hazel was so rude to you and forced you to walk behind, too. I'm sorry about the whole thing. It was meant to be a pleasant visit.'

Rachel shrugged and said calmly, 'Why get bothered about such things? They're friends and neighbours. I'm only your secretary,' but she could see he was furious about it.

'I wish I didn't have to give the beastly June 1st Ball. But the social list seems to be a condition of the inheritance.'

'Oh, well, in that case, there's no point in my worrying about the list of engagements. I'll give it to you when we get back.'

'Why were you worrying?' he asked, curiously.

'It's a long list,' she said, pushing back her headsquare in a curiously comic gesture and wiping her hot forehead. 'There's the Vicar's Garden Party, the Flower Show, and the vicar (who is by way of being an enthusiast about getting on the right side of trendy young people) gives what he calls a Pop Revival but is in the nature of a competition in pop dancing and peculiar instruments and was always judged by your uncle. There's the competition for the best play for the local dramatic societies for twenty miles around — '

'Just a minute! Are you sure you're not inventing all this?'

Rachel looked amused. 'That's not a quarter of it. Are you good at opening things, making the graceful speech, judging things without fear of awful consequences from the unlucky losers afterwards?'

'You're getting at me!' He couldn't believe it.

'I assure you, it's all true. How come you didn't know? Where were you, all the time you lived here and these events took place?' she wanted to know.

'Hidden in my lab or taking healthful walks in the hills,' he said shortly. 'And how did you know all this?'

'Your solicitor gave me the information over the telephone.'

'When? How was it he wasn't put through to me?'

'Because I'm the one to type the information. Besides, you see him when he comes in person. The phone calls were for me. Two of them,' she added, not meeting his eyes. 'Never mind your solicitor — what about this cousin Amelia? I thought you didn't like her? Aren't you afraid her red-headed daughter will turn up too?'

Keith looked at the glitter of amusement in her eyes. She was learning more about him every day. Now she saw that he didn't shout in anger like other men, but his eyes smouldered, and a small nerve twitched at the corner of his mouth. He had taken a stand for once, and she was making him feel an idiot, and most of all, hitting at his pride.

Rachel saw she had gone too far, but she had things on her mind, too. She tilted her chin at him and said, 'If I am to be the sort of pampered creature who is not only housekeeper and secretary but companion as well, then I am afraid you'll have to be prepared for me to be rather blunt. You haven't minded so far.'

His anger evaporated, puzzlement taking its place. 'I know that. But why all this *feeling* about this red-headed girl that you've never met? She might be quite as horrid as I think she is. You seem to be taking a marked interest in her. Why?'

Rachel turned her head away. 'You seem to be such a well-balanced person. This girl's your Achilles heel. I suppose I don't like it in you. That's all.'

'You think I'm unjust,' he said,

shrugging. He didn't like it.

It was unfortunate that they ended the conversation like that. They were both so busy after that, and it was some little time before he realised that it wasn't just pressure of time that prevented more talks with Rachel. She was avoiding him.

The sight of her empty desk made him lonely, when he emerged from the lab. He missed the sight of that grey head bent over the papers, and the trick she had of looking up and quickly pushing up her spectacles, as if she hadn't been using them to work with. An endearing quality in Rachel. She must have been fun to know, before her hair went grey, he thought.

One day he began to search for her. She wasn't consulting with or speeding up her excellent band of male house-workers. He caught sight of her with Hugh, the estate agent, in the Land-Rover. They were throwing back their heads, laughing together, before the Land-Rover went out of sight behind a clump of trees. Keith remembered seeing Rachel quietly laughing with Neville Shaw the last time he had come down. Was she telling them about her home life, her childhood, her previous jobs — a thing she had resolutely refused to tell Keith himself?

A wave of different anger swamped him and he saw it as no less than jealousy. He was shocked at himself. He dare not press her for more details about herself: she had already threatened to leave, if he did. He knew only too well that he couldn't bear the thought of her leaving him.

He was thinking on these lines, uneasily giving half of his attention to what the Colonel was saying. Colonel Radlett was a difficult person to keep at arm's length. He just couldn't believe that a nephew of his old friend, Edward Chilton, didn't love horses.

'Why do I have to re-open the stables?' Keith asked in pure exasperation one day. 'Honestly, I regard riding as a thing expressly robbing me of time in my lab.'

'Can't stay bending over test tubes all day, my boy,' the Colonel said, outraged. 'Besides, must ride, if you re-open the stables. If you don't re-open the stables, it might suggest economy, dear boy. The Grange has never exhibited anything so vulgar as economy before. Bad show!'

Money. Everyone referred to it, in some way or another. Keith, who had had so little before, now found it an enormous responsibility and a time-wasting responsibility at that. Neville Shaw came down with great sheafs of papers to be gone through, and if Keith succumbed to the temptation of turning the job over to Rachel, he suffered new torments, seeing her head close to that of his solicitor, who was a big handsome well-set-up man in his late forties, who seemed to find plenty to laugh over in an intimately quiet way with Rachel. The intimacy that envelops those involved in checking important work, a kind of shutting out of the world in a mutual fog of concentration and interest. Keith didn't like it at all.

'Why can't all this wait until if and when I inherit it?' Keith would demand in sheer frustration.

Neville merely smiled and remarked, 'I think you soon will be owning it, from what I hear,' and then he'd start to talk about Melanie and her knowledge of horses, and her infinite suitability as a wife for Keith, and of how much his uncle would have approved.

Keith, protesting always that he hadn't made up his mind, was aware that the bloated indoor and outdoor staff were speculating. It was little different from when there had been female staff as in his uncle's day, and lively speculation grew with the frequency of the visits of father and daughter.

Out of Rachel's list of social events, the day of the gymkhana stood out in Keith's mind. A hot day. Everybody had predicted rain, but it didn't rain, and Keith, watching all the activity, preparing the field with the jumps and fences, wondered how he had managed to escape all this when his uncle was alive. Now he was forced to be here, and had no need to do a single thing, he found watching the preparations rather fascinating.

He didn't know whether to be amused or ashamed at his own ignorance, considering he was the one supposed to be organising all this. He listened to some small children discussing the erection of the jumps for the first jumping event.

Carol Harris, with three small children in tow, belonging to her brother, came up and stood by him, pleased to find Keith unmonopolised. 'Do you know anything about it?' she asked softly. She was laughing at him. In spite of the clothes put out for him by his excellent man, he didn't really look the part, he knew.

He said indignantly, 'I am not

entirely ignorant, I hope I am aware that for this event the five jumps are a box-hedge, a gate, a wall, a stile, and a triple bar,' and as her eyebrows shot up in some surprise, he added, laughing, 'Well, I heard two half pints the age of those of your brother's, discussing it. How old are those, by the way?' he asked, looking at her nephews and niece. He was depressed to hear they were all under ten, and as confident as they looked.

He hoped she'd go away when the three children mounted and entered the next event, but she stayed by him. 'Are you judging, by any chance?' she gently teased, and laughed when he indignantly said, 'You must know I'm only the chap who pins the rosettes on, and I doubt if I'll do that without botching it.'

Hazel Masters finally ousted Carol from his side, by presenting the four small riders from her own family, and bringing her parents to speak to him. Melanie, spotting him from the other side, brought her father over, and he was the centre of an uneasy competition for his personal favours. He wished Rachel were with him. She would have explained everything without making him feel so out of it all.

Hazel's smallest nephew fell and she left his side at once, her parents going with her, to edge their way to the point where the riders left the field. The little boy was covered in mud and fell off twice more and was disqualified.

Melanie reluctantly left his side to help the children of friends who were staying at the Radlett house, and Carol was left victorious. 'Did you know my grandmother attended this right up to the last?' she murmured. 'Gran would be glad to know you were carrying on the tradition, Keith.' She twinkled at him and said, 'But frankly I don't think you're enjoying it!'

Melanie had come back. 'Of course he is!' she snapped, and the two girls glared at each other. But Melanie was out of luck. The vicar bore her off to meet someone and Keith was left with Carol again.

She seemed to be different today, out of that studio of hers, with no make-up on, no streaks of paint or clay on her clothes. She was neatly turned out in reasonable jodhs and boots, a well-fitting jacket, and she carried her crop in rather a dashing way. Her hair wasn't loose, either, but tidily hidden under her hard velvet cap and he found that he disliked her less than Melanie, who kept returning with a proprietory air that irritated him.

It was an exhausting day for Keith. He couldn't understand why it should be so, when a spell in Casualty at his old hospital had left him fit and deeply interested. He supposed it was the tension beneath the polite faces of the three young women. He noticed that Carol's eyes were a very light grey and her voice light and hard, her diction clipped, inclined to be staccato. She could fling a child up expertly into the saddle, but how would she be with a sick child, he wondered? How would Melanie be, if a child caught the dread disease, and she was called upon to help — how far would that rather low smooth voice of hers get her? A seductive voice, but not a voice to soothe a child in a raging fever. And Hazel?

What was he doing here, he asked himself? What had his uncle intended? How could you tear yourself in two, be a social animal, choose a wife, in order to secure, by such back-door means, the wherewithal to continue work that was demanding, terribly disappointing and elusive at best, but work that was so urgently needed? Where was the sense of it all?

Pressingly, absurdly, he wanted Rachel. Melanie was saying, 'You really should have made an effort, Keith. Your uncle actually made it his business to know the names of every child entrant and the individual form!' but all Keith could think of was that Rachel was avoiding him. Why, why?

And what was his cousin Amelia doing? Why hadn't she continued to pester him about her daughter being missing?

It was later that day, when he went back to the house, the trophies duly presented by him and the appropriate things said — that he found there had been a telephone message from his cousin.

'THERE HAS BEEN A LETTER LEFT BY LYDIA TO SAY SHE WAS INTENDING TO GO FOR A HOLIDAY WITH FRIENDS BUT IT MUST HAVE BLOWN DOWN UNDER A PIECE OF FURNITURE AND HER FLAT MATE HAS ONLY JUST FOUND IT,' Amelia had said.

The message had been typed by Rachel, who was back at her desk.

Keith, who only liked talking to people about things that mattered, such as sickness and pain, was exhausted by the number of senseless social remarks he had had to answer and comment on that day. He screwed the message up and threw it at the waste paper tub, remarking, 'Thank heavens for that! The wretched girl appears to have been located. Now I can have some peace in *that* quarter at least!' but he surprised a stormy look in Rachel's eyes. The same sort of hostility as there had been when he had mentioned Lydia's red hair on that other occasion.

He threw himself into a chair and stared at Rachel, but she ignored him and went on typing at that fantastic speed of hers.

'Rachel, stop working! I want to talk to you!' he commanded.

'Yes?' she said icily. She hated being interrupted.

'Why didn't you come out and see the gymkhana with me?'

She half smiled. 'Too much work. Too many past gymkhanas. They're all very much alike. Besides, you had some enthusiasts around you, surely?'

'That's not the point,' he answered, nettled. She made him feel like a petulant child. 'I wanted *you*.'

He dragged himself to his feet and

went over to her desk, leaning on it to look into her eyes. He always felt, when she had left him, that he might have found the answer to a lot of things if he had remembered to have a closer look at her before she replaced those tinted glasses of hers.

She probably sensed his intention, for she looked down, murmuring, 'Do you mind awfully if I go on working while you're talking?'

'Yes, dash it, I do. I want to discuss this with you. Why don't we go out together any more?'

'I wasn't aware that we ever did,' she said frigidly. 'You showed me over the estate, as I would expect as a newcomer, and that was the end of it.'

'No, it wasn't. Besides, we lunched together first, and you agreed you would be a companion to me.'

'The inference was, if I had time,' she said mildly. 'And I haven't.'

'Well, *make* time!' he said heatedly. 'There are things I want to discuss with you.'

She looked at him in exasperation. It was like when, as a small boy, he had bothered an elderly aunt with his questions, and her voice and manner had been just like this. He waited for Rachel to say something as crushing as his old aunt had done, but she merely remarked, 'Verena West, the actress, telephoned.'

It completely surprised him. He had forgotten all about her. 'What on earth did she want?' and he sounded more interested than he had meant to.

'She says she'll be passing here on the way to some function or other and wonders if she could look in on you.'

'Well, yes, I suppose so,' he said, impatient now. 'Never mind about her. I want to talk about you. Could we go somewhere tomorrow?'

To his fury, Rachel gravely considered the point, consulted the diary beside her, and produced a convincing list of things she had to do that couldn't possibly be put off. 'How about next week?' she suggested kindly, but there was amusement in her eyes. 'Are you surprised I'm so busy?' she asked him. 'It's your uncle's list of social functions, you know.'

'But you have to stop to eat. Don't you want to come out to dinner with me?' he asked bluntly.

She sat back, abandoning all attempt at work. 'Look, won't it look a little odd for *you* to be seen taking *me* out to dinner?'

'I don't see why,' he said, and the more she made it difficult, the more he wanted to arrange it.

Finally, she said with devastating frankness, 'There are some people who might say that I'm old enough to be your mother.'

Now he came to look at her, she did look much older and she had a lot of make-up on, too. Lines from her eyes, and down by her mouth, made him wonder if he had imagined that smooth face and unlined pair of eyes the day she had had that meal with him. But it made no difference. It was her personality that tugged at him. He said, 'I don't quite see . . . ' and then added bluntly and quickly, before her attention wandered back to her work, 'Is it possible that you don't want to come out with me?'

'Well, let me think about it, can I?' she said kindly, after an obvious pause that bothered him.

He walked away, frustrated; aware that his feelings towards her worried him as much as they did her.

The vicar came later to discuss two of the items on the list — that hated list of social functions Keith was forced to comply with. Rachel had typed six copies of it, so that, he thought, he would be quite unable to use the excuse of losing the list. He showed a copy to the vicar, on impulse.

'Is this really a list, a true list, of all the things my uncle did?' Now he would know, he told himself.

The vicar studied it and said definitely, 'No.'

'Ah, I thought not,' Keith said, with satisfaction.

The vicar dashed his satisfaction by saying quickly, 'Your uncle had a much longer list. This appears to have been much shortened. Aren't you intending to do everything, dear boy?'

Keith felt caught. He felt just as trapped where Melanie was concerned, too. He hadn't noticed until now, that Melanie and her father worked as a team, turning on charm, but putting Keith in such a position that he found he had to keep giving way to their suggestions every inch of the way, otherwise he would have appeared ill-bred, rather a boor. In extreme irritation he suddenly realised that he was getting far less work done in his laboratory than if he had had to pack it all up and move out, settle it in some far less suitable position. In fact, he began to wonder whether it wouldn't be better to pack up and go, now. This social round was his biggest enemy, and it had crept up on him.

It was in this frame of mind that he found it had been arranged for him to go out to dinner with the Colonel, Melanie and two friends of theirs, and the Colonel's sister — a woman Keith had never liked because her flowing apparently well-bred conversation was full of pitfalls for him. He was shocked, too, to discover that this engagement had been arranged by Rachel.

'Did you really arrange this for me?' he demanded.

He had found her in the still-room, a workmanlike notebook in one hand, and a biro in the other. She turned and gave him her full attention. 'Yes. Wasn't it right?' she asked coolly.

'You know dashed well it wasn't. You must know I'd get out of a party like this as soon as I could.'

'Well, from what the Colonel said, I gathered it was something you particularly did want on this occasion. I'm sorry. Shall I cancel it? And what shall I say, by way of a reason?'

'Oh, don't be so absurd. I shall have

to go now! And what will *you* do while I'm gone?'

She looked at him with such an odd look. 'The same as I do any other night, I expect — read a book.'

The Colonel was to call for Keith, in his big car with the rest of the party. Keith prowled restlessly, uncomfortable in white tie and tails, uneasily certain that his need for Rachel's friendship was making him moody and irritable with everyone.

He went down to the library, deciding he'd ask her how he looked. The great room was in shadow. A pool of light, as usual, was on her desk, but she wasn't sitting at it, just standing near. He said, 'What are you in the dark for? How do I look?'

She came across the shadowed room to him. 'Your tie isn't straight — shall I do it for you?' she said.

She had to stand on tiptoe to do his tie and he noticed at once something unfamiliar about her: she had perfume, a teasing whisper that was vaguely exciting. She wasn't in her usual working clothes, either, but before he could turn her round to the light and study her, someone got up out of the shadows. It was Neville Shaw, his solicitor, also in white tie and tails.

'What the devil are you doing here,' Keith demanded.

Neville Shaw laughed. 'You don't mind, do you? I heard you'd be out tonight, so I came down to collect Rachel to take her to London,' he said easily. 'She's got through that mountain of work and she hasn't anything else to do.'

Keith stared at Rachel, who had diplomatically turned on all the lights. She was in a long grey lace dress, the last word in elegance, and yet it somehow didn't look right on that slender girlish figure of hers. He found himself wishing she'd put on a pretty dress, a dress for someone younger. Something had been done to that short grey hair and she had a pearly ornament in it, which matched the ear-rings and a rather unusual necklace of pearls and garnets, and she was quite unsmiling.

'I didn't think you'd mind,' she said at last, to Keith, 'if I went out too, as you won't be in. You did ask me what I'd be doing but at that time I was only planning to read a book.'

'You sure you don't mind Rachel spending the evening with me, dear boy?' Neville Shaw asked easily, coming to stand rather possessively, it struck Keith, just behind Rachel.

Did he mind! Keith said, between his teeth, '*Where* are you taking Rachel?'

'Oh, I thought I'd take her to dinner and perhaps a show. We can get back from London easily before your party, I expect. Are you sure you don't mind?' he repeated, and Rachel was looking as if she really wanted to know if Keith minded.

'No, why should I?' Keith said unwillingly. 'She's her own mistress, I suppose. It's just damned odd that if I hadn't come in here to speak to Rachel,

I wouldn't have known.'

'That's true,' Neville agreed, infuriatingly. 'I didn't think it was necessary to mention it to you. We've been out once or twice when you've been dining over at the Colonel's place. Rachel gets her work done. She has to have some time off sometimes. She tells me you haven't arranged any.'

Keith flushed. 'She only had to ask me about it but she never did.'

Rachel broke in, in a bored tone, 'Oh, can we leave it? I think I heard the Colonel's car drive up just now,' so Keith went.

But he knew he wasn't going to enjoy the evening at all. He kept thinking of them as he had seen them: Neville getting up lazily out of his deep armchair and standing behind Rachel like that, and they made a handsome couple. Neville was about forty-five, extremely well set up; his tailoring was so good, he looked as if he had been poured into that suit. And he looked, too, as if it was his concern what happened to Rachel that evening, and Rachel — Keith remembered — had looked quite contented if not exactly happy, that that should be the way of things.

4

Rachel waited nervously to see what would be the outcome of the engaging of the cousin Amelia as hostess for the June 1st Ball. Keith was unapproachable because of all the time lost in his lab. Finally, after managing to get a long uninterrupted period of work done there, to his satisfaction, Keith changed his mind. 'We'll have Simon's fiancée Joan to be hostess,' he pronounced, quite unaware that Rachel breathed more freely after that.

Joan was quite happy to accept. It was now almost half way through the period given to Keith in which to find a wife and so inherit the estate. Neville Shaw was getting edgy, but when he talked to Rachel about it, she was curiously unco-operative.

'What you're asking is for me to edge him towards a choice.'

'Well, my dear, you like him enough to know it would break him up to lose the house and all it means to him, surely?'

She avoided Neville's eyes. She didn't want him to know just what her feelings for Keith were. 'I'm the general factotum and I enjoy smoothing his path, through my work, but I don't choose a life's partner for him, nor will I plot to bring it about. Well that's what you want, isn't it?'

'Yes, I suppose I do,' Neville said slowly. 'I thought I was a good judge of character and that you'd play ball. I just wonder why you won't.' But she wasn't to be drawn.

All was bent towards getting ready for the Ball. The big social event of the district. The weather was hardly conducive to a summer ball. All through May it had rained so much that part of the village had been flooded but the Grange escaped, standing on such high ground.

Keith refused to think about the Ball.

It was impossible to avoid Melanie's company without giving offence but he refused to talk to her about the first day of June.

They paused at the top of the rise looking down on the Pond Cottages early one morning. There was still damp in the air and thick mist clung to the hollows but it was a peerless time for riding. Even Keith, no lover of horses, allowed that. But he was a poor companion to someone like Melanie.

'Doesn't it thrill you to own all those wonderful animals?' she demanded, looking round into his face persuasively.

He wasn't even looking at her. His eyes were on the Pond Cottages. 'No, frankly no,' he said absently.

'You're thinking about your laboratory,' she accused him. 'You've never told me — what exactly *do* you do in there all those hours?'

'Well, you must know what a lab looks like, from schooldays. How good were you at physics and chemistry?'

She pulled an expressive face.

'Well, then, how can I begin to tell you?' he reasoned.

'I suppose you sit at a high stool all the time and look at nasty wriggling things through a microscope,' she guessed. 'I suppose if I can't persuade you to move away from here, you'll be wanting to fish about in that ghastly pond for specimens? Well, I should think there are enough diseases in that stretch of water to keep you busy with your little microscope for the rest of your life!'

'Yes,' he said slowly, and without thinking, began to move slowly down towards the pond.

Melanie caught at his bridle imperiously. 'Oh, no, you don't, Keith! We're out for a nice healthful ride, accent on the healthful. And when — that is, whoever you choose for your wife, I shall see that she first of all gets that lot cleared away — the hovels, the pond, the lot! For everyone's sake!'

He didn't appear to notice her first slip. He was thinking of the rest of what she had said, and he looked at her. He had a curiously direct look, before which her eyes fell away. 'Come on, race you to Blacketts End,' she said, and whacked his horse's rump as well as her own.

But later he thought of that incident, and remembered how Rachel had looked professionally at the rash on the faces of those children. He had forgotten to take it up with her. He promised himself that he would do.

Melanie put it out of his mind, however, with talk of the Ball. 'You know it's as important as the Christmas festivities hereabouts, of course?'

He shook his head, rather bewildered, and wanting to keep on thinking about Rachel.

'Don't you know what it's in aid of?' Melanie demanded, but when he allowed that he didn't, she laughed and wouldn't tell him. He decided to tackle Rachel about that, too.

The frosty atmosphere between Keith and Rachel, however, since the evening she had spent in London with his solicitor, had intensified between them and the longer it went on, the more difficult it seemed to stop it. Rachel had reverted to taking her meals in the housekeeper's room, and in many ways Keith found himself blocked when he wanted personal conversation with her. But on the day following that ride with Melanie, he did find Rachel alone in the library. It was not the day for his solicitor to come, and the estate agent, he knew, had gone to Melmerstead. He stood squarely in front of Rachel's desk, but he didn't say what he wanted to, because she looked different.

He knew nothing of make-up, stage make-up, or the way the hair and clothes could make a woman look younger or not so young. He only knew that Rachel looked much older today. 'Is this because of my solicitor?' was all he could think of to say.

'Is *what* because of your solicitor?' she asked, surprised.

'All that stuff on your face. It makes

you look terrible. Years older,' and he hated himself.

'Oh, that,' she said. 'Well, if he likes it, what does it matter?' but she looked curiously satisfied, when Keith had expected her to be furious or indignant.

She turned back to her notes, so Keith brought up a chair and sat facing her. 'Rachel. Look at me! What's the matter? What's gone wrong between us?'

She was going to be mulish, difficult, he could see. 'I don't understand,' she said at last.

'Now don't play stupid. You must know what I mean. I didn't — I couldn't have imagined it. We got on so well together at first. It's all changed. Have you taken against me for something?'

'No, I don't think so,' she said, indifferently.

'Then why don't we have those jolly talks any more?'

'Because of the way you looked at me that night when I went out with your solicitor,' she said impatiently. 'You didn't like it, did you? Why didn't you say so?'

He shrugged. 'Bad enough not to want you to go with him.'

'Why didn't you want me to go out with him?' she pressed.

He couldn't stop staring at her. She had a fine wool sweater on against the damp chill of this unfriendly late May day, with a high polo neck, and he thought it was mainly to hide new wrinkles showing darkly in her neck. He flushed a little. It was unpardonable of him, and no business of his what his secretary wore or looked like, but it was almost as if she was a relative of his, he felt so protective towards her, and she *was* looking so much older. The doctor in him needled him on that score. He said, 'Are you all right? Are you well?'

Aggravating she said 'Yes' and waited.

'You don't look awfully well,' he frowned, and wondered how he could suggest examining her without provoking a storm. If she'd only take off those tinted glasses so he could see how her eyes looked! He got the feeling that the eyes would tell him the truth.

'Well, I'm sorry,' she said smartly. 'I can't help how I look and it wasn't in the agreement — I am feeling as vigorous as usual and getting through as much work. Have you any complaints about my work?'

'No, it's not that,' he frowned. 'It's just that you don't look the same as when you first came,' and now he recalled that almost always her voice was the voice of an older person, but sometimes it unaccountably had the gaiety and vigour of someone much younger. Almost as if she were acting. But then, his thoughts tumbled about, she *was* an actress, wasn't she?

She watched him, narrowly. Half of her was amazed that he hadn't seen through it all before now, and the other half of her didn't want him to start guessing. Besides, there was Neville behind her, wanting her to push a marriage forward, and she didn't want to do that either.

To take Keith's mind off the present subject and to stop him looking at her in that disconcerting way that made her heart thump uneasily, she said, 'You didn't even ask me what I did that evening in London or whether I enjoyed it.'

'Is it too late to ask now?' he drove himself to say.

She shrugged. 'Your solicitor entertained me royally and he wants to make another date. The opera this time.'

She didn't sound as if she were interested. 'Do you like it?' he asked blankly. 'I wouldn't have thought opera — '

She shrugged again. 'Not very much. But I'll go. I like being wined and dined and entertained, as well as the next person.' And then, as his face changed and she saw he was going to suggest taking her out himself, she said quickly, 'What's happening about your forthcoming marriage? Neville's getting anxious.'

Neville. All the jealousy in him rose and threatened to choke him, hearing her use his solicitor's christian name, yet she refused to call him Keith. She avoided using a name at all.

He pushed back his hair. 'Nothing's happening. I haven't even thought of it.' He leaned forward, yearningly, almost, as he began to tell her what had been happening in his lab. 'If I could have kept awake one more hour I think I would have had a breakthrough. It's as near as that.'

Rachel struggled to keep the enthusiasm out of her face and voice, as she forced herself to say what she must. 'Then if it's that near, hadn't you better take the plunge and do something to ensure that you are able to keep your lab as it is? Surely you don't want an upheaval at a time like this?'

He looked as if he had had a bucket of ice water thrown in his face. He had just been going to tell her what he felt about those children at the Pond Cottage, and to ask her point blank if she had ever been a nurse; it had suddenly looked enticing, the thought of Rachel sharing his hours in the lab at this critical time, when he was on the brink of discovering something.

He was moved to say so, but as always, she said something to stir that restrained anger of his. 'Also time's running out. And if I may say so, you are seeing so much of Miss Radlett that the district has already made up its mind that she is to be the one.'

It was a sure-fire winner, Rachel thought sadly, as a dull flush ran up his cheeks and he marched out of the room.

She covered her face with one hand, and blinked hard against the tears that stung her eyes too much lately. And then she looked in disgust at her hand and decided she'd have to re-make-up. It always amazed her that he was so lost in his own unhappy world of chasing that particular bug, that he didn't even realise the significance of her never looking really the same two days running. And she, poor idiot, had let her emotions run away with her!

She thought of him now, having escaped back to his lab. He would have forgotten her, put on his white coat, and sat down at his notes again.

But he hadn't. He stood in the centre of all that extravagance that his uncle had provided for him, and he couldn't work. He was restless, miserable, yearning for heaven knew what. Somehow it tied up with Rachel who was, so she had said from time to time, old enough to be his mother. Today she looked it, in those dreadful clothes and with all this new make-up on, which didn't help her appearance at all. But somehow, today, something didn't seem quite right. If only he could get close to her, to really look at that face of hers. But she was as elusive as a wild animal, and after all, she was only an employee; he could hardly insist.

Irritated, he went and sat down and tried to work, but he kept thinking of the way she had looked, that day they had had lunch together. She had seemed so young in herself. Young and vital and just the sort of person he wanted near him all the time. Absurdly he wanted to push time back to that day again. He pushed his notes away. Why shouldn't he insist on seeing her birth certificate, all the other things an employer had the right to ask to see? But she was hiding such details for some reason, and if he insisted, Keith knew that it would do no good. She would just pack up and leave him, and he couldn't endure the thought of that.

★ ★ ★

The pelting rain kept on until two days before the Ball and then a hot spell set in. It was so curiously breathlessly hot, it was ridiculous to imagine that the weather could have changed so quickly in such a short time. The lawns steamed where the water had been lying and he wondered how they were going to arrange to have dancing outside. But the sun's heat did its work on well-drained lawns, and the day that he had been dreading so much. The giant motor mowers were now still, and the countless people who had moved purposefully about in their business of setting up this Ball, had gone. He thought of the sight of Rachel, little determined grey-haired bespectacled Rachel, organising the whole thing. Directing furniture removers here, and caterers there; people taking instructions from her with respect, following her brief but knowledgeable comments and looking as if they really liked working with her. While he, Keith, was kept, as usual, at a distance from her.

Keith wondered again why his uncle had kept up this annual money-wasting permanent social date. He was a serious young man who saw life as a kaleidoscope of countless very sick people suffering from bugs that were almost if not quite unknown, and a few people like himself, sitting at benches, testing, fighting, straining to discover a cure.

His uncle admitted the seriousness of his nephew's ambition, indeed, had he not gone a long way to equip his nephew, but in leaving this problematical Will, it was as if his uncle was saying, at the same time, that hand in hand with the sick and the people who would cure them, must be the ones who dispensed gaiety and those who were able to enjoy it.

But for Keith, it wasn't reason enough. It seemed that the whole county was coming, their primary object to be there when the announcement was made, and to know whom he would choose as his bride. This really was of some great interest to them. If it was to be one of the local people, they would be much happier. There was always fear that it might be someone from London, with no interest in country affairs.

As he received the guests, standing at Joan's side, he wondered what had happened to Rachel. He was disappointed. The last time he had seen her, she was on the delicately carved sweep of the main staircase, unfamiliar now with its tubs of flowers. Rachel had seemed so used to directing all this sort of thing, he had been impelled to ask her what experience she had had, but that slightly malicious gleam of amusement in her eyes prevented him from doing any such thing. And now she was nowhere to be seen, but Joan was occasionally giving him oblique glances of encouragement, smoothing the way for him. She was used to this sort of thing, too; her father was a widower.

He was just going to escape from it all when Joan quietly put it to him that he would now have to dance, every dance. He was the host. 'And if I might give a word of warning,' she added in a comical whisper, 'don't dance more than once with any girl if you don't like her specially, because you know what you are here for, and everyone will start thinking things.'

It was difficult to carry out such good advice where Melanie was concerned, and then he saw Rachel, in that mature grey lace creation he had seen her in before. She was, of course, dancing with Neville, a little too close to him, Neville Shaw looking handsome and possessive. Keith smouldered with anger.

He missed her soon afterwards. Hazel, dancing with him, asked, 'Who are you looking for, Keith?' and she sounded offended.

He was shocked to think that he had betrayed his thoughts in such a way. Trying to be casual, he said, 'If you must know, I'm wondering what on earth I'm going to do, if and when I inherit this place, if I've got to give parties like this all the time.'

Hazel's face cleared. 'Oh, is that all? Don't worry, you'll get used to them. You'll even start to enjoy them. After all they don't happen every night, you know.'

He said defensively, 'Do you know what my life is like? I spend most of it in the laboratory.'

It was meant to be off-putting, but

Hazel merely murmured, 'Like me. I expect to spend most of my life with sick animals. There isn't any reason why that shouldn't continue, is there?' A clever answer which tricked Keith into thinking he had been afraid for nothing.

It was after this that he stumbled on Rachel, in the library. He'd gone there to escape the noise. He found Rachel standing quietly at the window, at one end of the long room, staring out at one of the few views, tonight, that wasn't lit and invaded by guests. The dark garden against a sky that lit occasionally with summer lightning was infinitely soothing, and she turned with a rather 'caught' expression. 'I was only looking at the weather,' she said. 'I think it's going to be a storm.'

He pulled her into the light and looked down at her face again. This was the nearest she had ever let him get to her and he was surprised to see that hideous make-up was no longer there. He traced her face with one finger. It was smooth, *young*.

Alarmed, she pushed away from him. 'What are you doing, *sir*?' she said, with all the frigidness that she might have shown if he had tried to make unwelcome love to her. 'Do you usually go on like this with your secretaries?' She was frightened, not at him but at the way her heart was behaving. His nearness did things to her that she had experienced with no other man, and it wasn't as if he were the flirty type, she thought helplessly.

'I don't know,' he answered her. 'I've never had one before, and to be honest, I'd never want one again if you ever left me. There's something about you, Rachel, that I don't understand.'

She turned from him. 'I think,' she said, 'that you'll be much better settled when you've got your inheritance and you can plan your life as you want to. It must be dreadful going on like this, not knowing what's going to happen and when. I do understand how you feel, and nobody wants to see you settle down and inherit this house more than I do.'

He grunted and said, 'Well, thanks for your tender thoughts on my behalf. I really came to find you to ask you to dance with me.' But she refused.

'Well, *why* can't you dance with me? You're not waiting for somebody else, are you?' he persisted, so she answered reasonably.

'No, but I don't think it would be the thing, out there in full view of all those people who will look at you and wonder . . . well, you're supposed to be dancing with someone you might choose to . . . well, you're the cynosure of all eyes tonight.'

'Oh, if that's all, we'll dance in here,' he said. 'We can open the door a bit so we can hear the music,' so with a sigh she said, 'All right,' just as if dancing with him was something tiresome to be got over with.

It was a waltz. He didn't know why he had insisted on dancing with her. Whether it sprang from jealousy because his solicitor had taken her out for the evening, or from some other emotion he didn't understand. He was all upset inside. But as he had rather anticipated, whatever her age, whatever she was really like, they danced as if they had trained together over the years. As one. They fused together, they absolutely fitted each other, step by step. It was almost as if they were hypnotised into moving together. They danced, closely, slowly and beautifully, all round the heavy pieces of library furniture, and he caught a glimpse of her in one of the mirrors, her face upturned, her eyes closed, and the music had an almost trance-like effect on them both.

He didn't know quite what would have happened then, but quite suddenly the door was thrust open and Neville Shaw stood there, and he said, 'Good heavens, what's the matter? Isn't the ballroom good enough for you both?'

It shattered the mood, but in a way they were both very glad of the interruption, for it was strange and unreal, and Keith at least hadn't known what he was going to say or do next. He was rather afraid of what would have emerged from that incident. He was angry with himself for having pandered to his strange desire to dance with Rachel. He was quite sure she hadn't liked it.

This was strengthened by the way she nodded when Neville proposed the next dance, and she went straight away with him to the ballroom without a backward glance.

5

After that, the storm broke, and it was a really bad storm.

On the whole, that was the worst evening's entertainment of Keith's life. He didn't like people in the mass. He didn't like having to keep smiling and pleased to see people he'd either forgotten or didn't even know. His uncle wouldn't have been pleased with such thoughts, he was quite sure. But he had managed to look the perfect host, and inevitably — with pleasure-able bafflement as to who he would still decide to choose for his bride — people accepted the end of that long, long evening and began to go.

He had thought that now at last he could escape and relax, and the half thought was in his mind that he would go, not to bed but to his laboratory, when some of the guests returned and said it was not possible to get through the village because a tree had been struck by lightning and blocked the road and couldn't be moved until morning.

Rachel, Joan, Neville and the estate agent took charge, and Keith heard them finding out just who would be affected. Most of the guests could reach the motorway by routes left open. In fact the only people affected were three families, and of course, Melanie and her father were among them. So it was arranged that they should stay the night.

Keith, the perfect host, could have cried that he still had to be on his best behaviour. Melanie looked quietly satisfied, he noticed, that her good luck had held and that she was to be one of the people to stay at the Grange until morning.

He lost sight of Rachel. She had left and started making preparations for the extra guests. Keith just prayed that they'd all go to bed and leave him in peace.

He stood at last alone, at the window of his bedroom, all thoughts of escaping to the laboratory gone from his mind. He looked out at the lightning and listened to the crash of the thunder, and wondered uneasily if, as the owner of some fine new blood stock, he should be getting into suitable clothes and braving the elements to see if his horses were all right. He shrank from the task. The stable staff would be better at the job than he himself. Horses! He was quite sure that Melanie would be wanting to go down to them soon, and he wondered what would happen if she came and knocked on his door. What could you do with a girl who was so keen on horses?

As he stood there, absently watching the play of the lightning and the way the trees bowed down before the lashing wind and torrential rain, he thought of tonight. Curiosity had got the better of him and he had found out why the June 1st Ball had been held. His uncle, incurably romantic, had called it the Presenting Ball. Always, until tonight, there had been an engagement announced. The son or daughter of one of his friends, or even a young couple on the staff of his house or a pair from the village. Keith himself remembered hearing his uncle say that this Ball kept him young, and adding cynically that it also kept him popular. And so the old man had calculated that Keith's own engagement would be announced tonight.

Well, it hadn't, Keith told himself sourly. Perhaps for the first time he admitted that if he were to inherit the Grange it would have to be Melanie. He would, he supposed, shrink from her less than either Carol or Hazel. He didn't dislike the Colonel, and he could always be sure that his horses would be taken care of without any trouble on his own part.

He remembered Melanie, her dark hair gleaming, her silver dress making her conspicuous, although he hadn't liked its low cut. She had been laughing and happy, triumphant, as if she knew the outcome of his choice already. He thought of Carol Harris, rather splendid in brown velvet and old gold, looking equally happy and attractive, and Hazel Masters in a floral dress, almost stole the picture because she looked outdoor healthy, and natural. Two would be disappointed, anyway, and would they be hostile to his wife? If it were to be Melanie, she wouldn't care.

He was standing in the master bedroom. What, he asked himself, would it be like, having someone else sitting in front of that dressing-table, making up or whatever women do at night? A bachelor through and through, he shrank from the idea, and all he could think of, absurdly, was Rachel, hiding that grey hair under a silly boudoir cap one saw in advertisements, and making astringent comments on what had happened during the day. His mouth curved into a smile of sheer appreciation, and he was aware that, surprising as it might seem, he wasn't shrinking from the thought of Rachel in that position. Rachel in his bedroom was far, far less terrifying than any one of those three girls!

Now he was dealing with the subject at last, he saw that he had had no desire to kiss either Melanie, Carol or Hazel; no desire to see any one of them at his breakfast table each morning. They would chatter. He was never at his best first thing. But of course, he saw Rachel first thing every morning, and she was discreetly quiet, accepting that he didn't want to meet anyone so early. Rachel would be the only acceptable person to face after a particularly disappointing day in the lab or a day when his notes had all gone wrong and that book he was straining to write seemed as hopeless to put together as things could at times. Rachel . . .

Rachel alone understood his anxiety about the children at the Pond Cottage. Rachel alone understood the gnawing ache he got when he seemed no nearer to solving the riddle of the disease that had carried off a beloved aunt, the only mother he had known.

Those children at the Pond Cottages nagged at him. He had been over to look at them again. He had talked to the local doctor, who was busy and irritable and inclined to resent being questioned, as if his treatment of them had been at fault. It wasn't malnutrition: goodness, they were country bred, fed on home-grown vegetables and fruit, milk from the farm, their own eggs and hens. But there was a lethargy in their movements, he had noticed one day, when he had caught sight of them going into Wickenham Woods. That, and that disquieting rash up at the hairline . . .

It had been going on for a few minutes, that quiet tapping on his door. Aware of it suddenly, he put on the light and went across to open it, his heart beating absurdly fast. But what had he thought Rachel would want, at this hour, of him, he asked himself savagely, as he opened the door to find Arthur, in hastily donned sweater and slacks, his feet in tennis shoes.

'I'm sorry to disturb you, Mr. Keith, but Abney's at the door.'

'Abney?' Keith repeated, and now he was disturbed, to think that the father of some of those children should come here in the night, just when he'd been thinking about them. 'Is it the children?' he asked sharply.

Arthur, surprised, nodded. 'Wouldn't come here at this hour if he wasn't upset, sir,' he added, so Keith said, 'Has the local doctor been called in? How many of them are ill?'

'No, not ill, Mr. Keith. Missing. Only Abney thinks they're locked in the stables. That's where they've been lately. Keep sending them home, but they come back for some reason.'

'Wait while I get into something,' Keith said, and turned back to the room to find similar attire to his servant. What on earth did those children want to be in the stables for?

As he pulled on his sweater, Rachel's voice said, 'What's wrong? Is anyone ill?' so Arthur told her, and Keith looked eagerly at where she stood. It wasn't light in the corridor, but she looked young again. Touchingly young in a pale blue padded dressing-gown and little furry mules. Without her glasses, and with that hair covered, she had shed years.

She caught his intent glance, and scowled. 'I'll get dressed. If the guests wake they'll be wanting hot drinks,' and she shot out of his vision. He hurried into the corridor but she'd gone.

He sent Arthur to wake Ben, who was to be at hand if anyone else started wandering about, and then he stopped at the window at the end of the corridor which looked out on to the back of the grounds. There were people running about, lit by a pink glow that grew more lurid as he looked.

'Arthur! The stables are on fire!' Keith shouted.

Someone else — presumably Abney — muttered, 'It's them kids o' mine,' but from then on, there was no chance to think of any incident in isolation. Everyone's doors were flung open at the sound of Keith's shout, he supposed, and people began to get dressed. Ben shot past him to telephone for the fire engine but it had to come from the town.

He thought he saw Rachel, her grey hair gleaming like a silver cap, but if it was her, she was in a dark sweater and slacks and looked very little different from servants and guests who were all eager to go down and help. These were all horse lovers, Keith thought sourly.

He himself was thinking of the children, trapped in the harness loft.

Melanie called, 'The Silver Streak — he's so nervous. I'll go to him first.'

Her father was at the telephone as Keith ran through the lighted hall. The Colonel wasn't waiting for the town's fire engine. He was calling out people he knew from the village. Keith said over his shoulder, 'I thought someone said the road was blocked by a tree?' and he didn't wait to hear what the Colonel answered to that.

Melanie was well to the fore, giving directions. Keith saw, among the smoke and flames, dancing, high-spirited horses with cloth tied over their eyes, and his own stable staff taking directions from Melanie, whose voice was strong and curt, rather like a man's light-weight voice, but weighted by authority.

Keith went in and scrambled up the ladder and got down two of the children. One little girl was feebly crying. The boy was uncontrollably shaking. 'We didn't do it, mister, honest,' he was trying to say.

Melanie had got all the horses out and the stable staff were rushing about with buckets. Melanie said, 'Never mind the fire. Help me get these horses to safety,' and in the confusion the Colonel was giving advice that his daughter wasn't listening to, and the stable boys dropped more water buckets than they carried to the fire.

And then suddenly, as if a great blanket had been put over it all, the fire went out. Seth, the old groom, found Keith and said, in an admiring voice, 'See that, sir?' and absently took the third child from Keith's arms. 'That Miss Rachel, she's the one. Just climbed up, cut the rope, and down came the storage bales and smothered the lot, in one fell swoop. Thinks, she does. *And* makes no noise!'

'What? What storage? Where is she now?' Keith demanded, hurrying. He was dirty, and there was blood on him from where something sharp had torn at him, and he was desperately worried about this younger child who had started the fire.

A lot of people had come in from somewhere, and separated him from old Seth. Someone said they had rode or driven across the fields, avoiding the fallen tree. Melanie said, 'I've got the horses to safety, Keith. Goodness, what a good thing Daddy and I were here tonight. Your staff aren't much good! I must re-organise all this. It will never do. Come on, the storm's coming on again. Give those kids to Abney and let's get inside.'

There was a concerted rush to the house as the storm returned. The rain, which now fell like a cloudburst, would have been useful ten minutes ago but was now just a nuisance. He couldn't hear his own voice, as he tried to explain that he wanted the children brought into the house. People took them from him and put them in a waiting estate car, and he had to let them go, because he remembered he had no authority here, to insist on the children being put into bed for tests. Now he would have to go through all the system of approaching the parents to call in the local doctor, and hope he could have them admitted to hospital.

'Where's Rachel?' he demanded when he got into the house. Everyone was making a great deal of noise about getting into dry clothes and what they had done about the horses, and how the fire had been stopped.

'Damned bright idea on someone's part, to remember cutting that string would bring the whole damn lot down and smother the source of the fire,' the Colonel was telling someone, and clearly he thought it was his daughter's idea. 'Didn't know Melanie knew they were packed like that.'

'What were they?' someone asked him and the Colonel said, 'Sacks of fodder. Damned heavy stuff. They'll be ruined, of course, but this lad won't feel the draught over that,' and he laughed loudly at Keith.

'It was Rachel, my secretary, who thought of it,' Keith said, and the Colonel stared at him, as if he was affronted.

Melanie appeared, in dry clothes. She had heard that. 'Your *housekeeper*,' she corrected Keith sweetly, 'would do better to refrain from interfering — the idea, all these male servants! It was awful trying to get help to change. The maids will be reinstated at once. What your uncle would say —'

'Where is Rachel?' Keith repeated, tersely.

Melanie shrugged. 'Darling, does it matter? Go with the men into the library and get a drink. You look as if you needed one. No, perhaps you'd better find the First Aid Box and do something about your face. Come on, I'll help you. I'm supposed to be good at First Aid.'

Keith turned and hurried from her without a word. He caught Ben by the arm. 'Where's Rachel?' but neither Ben nor anyone else seemed to know.

Frustration and anxiety tore at Keith. He went out into the storm again, and over to the ruin of the left wing of the looseboxes. Seth and two of the hands saw him and came over with storm lanterns and helped him in his feverish dragging of the heavy bags away. Seth's jaw dropped as a girl's hand came into view, underneath them.

By the time Melanie had located the raincoats hanging in the garden room, and she and the others came streaming out, Keith was carrying Rachel into the house. He looked terrible. He marched ahead, and before that look on his face they fell back, leaving a gap for him to walk through, and nobody said a word about the streaming rain or the thunder, but the occasional sheet lightning lit the faces of them all and somebody said, 'Is she . . . still alive, d'you suppose?'

Joan and Simon followed Keith up to Rachel's room and Joan helped him to put Rachel down on the bed. She was limp as a doll, but all he could do was to stare at her.

'Shall I call a doctor?' Simon asked anxiously, but Joan said sharply, 'He *is* a doctor, aren't you, Keith? Well, you started out as one, I think,' and she, too, subsided into silence before the look on his face.

Rachel's eyes fluttered open, and Joan turned away in sheer embarrassment as

130

Keith slid to his knees beside the bed and gathered Rachel to him. Joan heard him say thickly, 'My heavens, I thought I'd lost you! I don't care what you're trying to hide, I can't . . . ' then he broke off as Simon made a movement at the door.

Joan brought a towel and started to mop Rachel's face, but Keith took it from her to do the job himself.

It was Melanie's voice, cutting through a murmur of voices that drew closer, coming up the stairs, that shattered everything. She was loudly demanding, 'But what's the *matter* with her, and is it really necessary for Keith to carry the housekeeper up to her bedroom?' and that, perhaps, did more to bring Rachel back to herself than anything.

'Keep her out,' she muttered, and struggled to sit up. 'What happened? Oh, yes, like a fool I fell off the beam! I remember! Sorry! I'm all right. The sacks weren't hard to fall on, only I knocked myself out on something, I think. Oh, don't fuss,' she said, pushing Keith away.

'But are you sure you're all right? I ought to — ' he said, with the vague intention of running over her to check for broken bones, but she said fiercely, 'Yes, I'm all *right*, I tell you! I've been a nurse. I know, don't I? Now, will you all please get out and leave me alone?'

Keith didn't seem able to tear his eyes away from her, though he got up. Melanie's voice was closer, and it spurred him into moving. He strode out as Melanie appeared at the door, and Joan heard him saying to her, as he urged Melanie downstairs in front of him, 'I want to talk to you, Melanie, in the library, private and personal — *now*. Yes, I'll tell you about Rachel later, but first I want to talk about *us*.'

Melanie stopped recriminating about what she termed 'a very odd business in the housekeeper's bedroom' and looked up sharply into Keith's face, in anticipation and pleasure, but Joan, who couldn't shut from her mind the agonised look in Keith's eyes as he had stared down at the unconscious Rachel, didn't think he was going to propose marriage to Melanie, or in fact say anything nice to her. He was a man in a fury, and it was worse because he was usually the most bland and good-tempered of men.

The rest of the house-party went to bed. It was anticlimax. All was quiet outside, except for the swishing of the steady downpour as the storm eased, reluctantly, but still hung around. The odd, occasional growl of thunder broke the silence, as Keith faced Melanie in the now cold library.

'Keith, darling, you're so impetuous,' she said, coming close to him. 'I appreciate this, but surely it could have waited until the morning?'

'No, Melanie, it can't,' he said, looking at her with a kind of cold surprise on his face. 'If I appear to be taking my time over this, it's merely because I want to put it as kindly as I can, while being as definite as possible.

You have said some things this evening, about re-organising things here in the future — '

'Oh, I am an idiot,' Melanie broke in, holding his arms and giving him a little shake. 'I get impatient. I don't mean anything. It was unpardonable of me to talk about re-organising the stables, and what I said about the maids. I don't even know that I care about the maids coming back. I was just irritated at the time, that's all.'

'Yes, but — ' Keith began, trying to marshal his thoughts.

'Think nothing of it, darling,' Melanie said firmly. 'I know you're a man's man and you wouldn't want things like the stables altered by your wife out of hand. We can talk it all over, much later. And I don't know that I want to change the house staff ever. Those male housemaids or whatever you call them are jolly efficient really.'

'I'm glad you think so,' he said stiffly, but again she broke in, this time not looking at him.

'But there's one thing I'll have to change, Keith, and you'll get used to it in time, but to be frank, no other woman would do anything else but change this either, no matter who you choose for your wife. I'm speaking of Rachel. She'll just have to go.'

She rubbed her cheek against his. 'If she doesn't, I'll start getting jealous of the attention you pay her, and that will be silly, considering she's no girl. Also darling, our friends might just think it a bit odd, you going so goo-ey over your grey-haired secretary,' and then she did look up at him, wondering why he still said nothing. 'Why are you looking at me like that, Keith?'

'It's what I'm trying to tell you,' he said patiently, yet with that chill in his voice which shocked her so. 'You're wonderful with horses. You come to life with horses. You saved the horses tonight . . . but you left Rachel to die.'

There was a marked pause, then Melanie said, 'I don't know what you're talking about. I don't know anything about Rachel. I'm not responsible for your staff, Keith.'

'Common decency should have made you go and find her to thank her for putting the fire out. Everyone around you was talking about how she did it. But all you were concerned with was getting in out of the rain. Even when I kept asking where she was, you didn't care.'

She whitened. 'That's right, I didn't care what happened to one of the staff. There are others to take care of them.'

'Well, I haven't been brought up to know how to go on, with a large indoor and outdoor staff,' he said coldly. 'I only know that my uncle looked after the welfare of each and every one of them as if they were old friends, and they came to him with their troubles and their pleasures. I would have thought common decency would put that into any employer's head. I'm sorry, Melanie, but the one I choose for my wife must care about people. Not only the staff, but people . . .'

'Like those scruffy kids from the Pond Cottages, who set fire to the stables and might have cost you a fortune in good new blood stock,' she finished bitterly.

'Yes, like those children,' he agreed, and walking to the door, he held it open for her.

She walked to the stairs. Joan was in the hall, waiting for someone. The sound of a car outside, and the slam of the door, made Joan walk briskly to the front door, but she couldn't reach the big top bolt, and looked round, chagrin in her face.

'Keith?' she said, so he left Melanie. Melanie heard Joan say, 'It'll be the doctor. I called him for Rachel — just in case,' and Melanie saw the smile that lit Keith's face, for Joan's action.

He undid the top bolt and she heard him talking to the village G.P. He and Joan had forgotten about her. All that mattered was that strange secretary of his, who sometimes looked all of forty, and sometimes a great deal less. Yes, a great deal less.

6

The doctor said there were no internal injuries but recommended a few days in bed, but Rachel wouldn't have that. She did, however, consent to rest on the swinging hammock in the sun lounge, a glassed-in place that Keith's uncle had had built as a sun trap after a run of wet cold summers.

Keith spent part of the day on the Abney children. In the mellow atmosphere of the Grange in the small hours, both men enjoying a brief drink before the doctor returned home, Keith took the opportunity, that night of the fire, to speak to him, not only about his fears that the children had the disease he was interested in, but also about his laboratory here at the Grange. Keith arranged to go and speak to Abney about the children the following morning in company with the doctor.

But that night the smallest child was taken ill and was admitted to the big glass and chromium hospital in Bexfield, which had its own isolation unit.

When Keith returned, in better understanding with the local doctor after discovering that both men had trained at the same teaching hospital in London though at different periods, Keith found that Rachel had a visitor. He halted, with his frosty look on his face. He had come back full of what had happened, all ready to tell Rachel about it, and here she was, apparently in close conversation with this florid-faced young man Keith vaguely remembered.

Rachel went pink and hastily introduced him as Tom Kelford. 'He's a friend of the Masters family. He was here last night with them,' she told Keith. She sounded faintly stiff, and Keith was decidedly stiff in his acknowledgement of the young man, who smiled easily and said, 'Well, hope you don't mind my popping over to see Rachel. Everyone's talking about how deuced brave and resourceful she was. In fact, everyone's talking about her, stat.'

'Why?' Keith and Rachel asked at the same time.

'Don't know, to be honest. They shut up when I hove in sight. Someone been putting something around. You know what villages are.'

'What has someone been putting around?' Keith snarled, to the surprise of both Rachel and her guest, who hastily said he hadn't an idea and perhaps he was mistaken, and if they'd excuse him he had another appointment.

After he'd gone, Keith said, 'I didn't like the look of that chap. Why did he come here, after only having met you last night?'

'What do you care?' Rachel asked, after a short silence.

Keith thought about it, then took the chair the guest had vacated and said quietly, with that old endearing manner of his that she loved so much, 'Rachel, I've had a rather nasty day and I came home to tell you all about it,' and her heart turned over at his choice of words. It sounded so nice.

'And what do I find,' he continued, 'but you entertaining a pompous horsey type like that chap. Well, all right, it's your business . . . I suppose. The fact is, I'm off horses and horsey types — the lot of them! — and that goes for Carol Harris and Hazel Masters, too. They'll both try to boss me and make me ride and go point to point, and show jumping, and judging little beasts on ponies and . . . What are you laughing at?' he broke off to ask.

If she hadn't laughed, she'd have cried, but she didn't tell him so. Instead, she said, 'What made today such a nasty day?' so he told her about the Abney children, the hospital, and his suspicions. As he had known would happen, her battling mood fled and she listened with great interest.

'Poor little wretches,' she murmured, 'and poor you, in a way. You're not ready for this, are you? I don't suppose they'll let you get near them, anyway. How long since you left hospital for private research?'

'Not long, a year,' he shrugged. 'But I left.'

She nodded, and there was that sudden intimacy in the air again. He said, without thinking, 'You've been a nurse, haven't you?'

He could have kicked himself for mentioning it, for he was quite sure that she hadn't meant to blurt it out the night before, and thinking she wasn't ready to disclose whatever she was hiding — probably some trouble connected with giving up nursing — he began to apologise.

'No, no, it's all right,' she said quickly. 'I only did the first year. I loved it. But it wasn't any use. I had to leave.' She shrugged. 'Family pressures. Don't ask me any more.'

He looked so distressed. 'I never

thought of you as having any family. Oh, help, that could complicate matters, I suppose.'

'How? What do you mean?' she sounded really alarmed.

He looked morosely down at her. 'I'm going to have an awful job telling you but I shall have to. It can't go on any longer.' He ran an agitated hand through his hair. 'First of all I terminated any hopes Melanie might have had. Last night. After I took her down from your room. No, don't start on at me about it. It was inevitable I was glad to be able to convince her. No, that isn't what I meant. I was going to tell her, after that wretched ball, anyway, only I couldn't have given anything else than lack of inclination as the reason, and that's not on, really, is it? But when she wasn't interested in finding you, only in saving the horses . . . well, I took her down to the library and explained about how my uncle looked after people and I'm like that, too, and I couldn't marry someone who cared more about horses than people in a crisis. It was as simple as that.'

'Oh, why did you have to?' Rachel moaned. 'Anything but that as a reason.'

'It's the truth,' he said simply. 'Anyway, I couldn't marry any one of those three girls, and today it came to me why. At the hospital, with the business of those Abney children, all I wanted to do was to hurry home and go over it with you. Now, I am quite sure that I would never feel like that towards Carol, say, or Hazel, if I'd married her. And certainly not to Melanie — but to you, yes! Don't you see, it's the perfect test! What are you staring at me like that for?'

'Because I don't know what you're talking about,' she said coldly. 'I'm just your secretary/housekeeper — ' she began.

He moved quickly, pushing her grey hair back with his hands at each side of her face, so that he couldn't see the colour of her hair, only her face cupped in his hands, and today she had no make-up on at all. Her face was smooth and clear. 'Rachel, what *is* going on?' he asked, puzzled and distressed. 'Is it a wig?'

'No, it isn't,' she snapped, jerking her head away. 'Now leave me alone while I think. You've only got three months left in which to get yourself married!'

He was still trying to pursue a thought about her but it eluded him so he gave it up for the time being, to tackle what she had said.

'Yes, I know, I've been thinking all round the subject, Rachel. We've been looking at young women, because my solicitor suggested that. Well, it was logical, I suppose. But does it have to be like that? I mean, I won't get anything but the inheritance out of such a marriage. And if I must marry, I want a wife who'll be . . . a companion to me,' he said, looking up at her with naked yearning in his eyes. 'Someone who'll give me what you give me: the desire to come home and confide, and you don't nag. You flare out if you're annoyed, but you're marvellous at making me laugh. Do you know how witty you are?'

'How did I creep into it again?' she asked, with weary patience. 'All right, we look for a wife for you who can be a good listener, keep you amused, not nag, but . . . '

'Shut up, Rachel,' he said quietly. 'I'm talking about you. I've been giving it quite a bit of thought. All right, as you keep reminding me — you are older than I am. What of it? Ill-assorted age groups make good couples. I don't know what your age is but we'll see that on your birth certificate, and meantime I recommend you to give up trying to use make-up. You're not good at it. It's disastrous when you put all that stuff on your face. It makes you look — well, it's much better like today, with nothing on your skin. You look almost young . . . '

'Thank you,' she said furiously. 'Perhaps you'd like me to dye my hair some bright colour and skip about and — '

He put a finger over her lips. 'Rachel, no matter what your age, you're the only one I can bear to be with every day, regardless of my moods and anxieties, regardless of whether it's work or leisure. Surely that's the answer? Isn't it, wouldn't you say? Or is it that I've been so obsessed with liking you that I've missed the point, that you don't like *me*?'

A little wind sprang up and moved a tree branch so that the sun shafted to her eyes. She threw an arm up over her face, to shield them, so he moved his chair so that his body came between her and the brightness, but she still didn't move her arm.

'Rachel, I wouldn't be impossible to live with. It could be just companionship, if you liked. I'm committed to my work, but I get very lonely. I foresee a very lonely life married to someone who didn't turn out to be compatible.'

Still she didn't answer, so he

continued, 'And it's not only that.' He took her other hand in his, and her heart smartened its pace uneasily. It would be so heavenly to fall in with his mood, allow herself to be tempted to agree to a marriage of companionship and then, when he'd got his inheritance, see what happened, let herself drift towards him in little ways . . .

But his next words crushed that thought. 'In a world of people who let one down sooner or later, you are the one, the only one, Rachel, that I feel I can trust. I know you'd never lie to me, or deceive me. Rachel, if you don't want to answer now, think about it my dear. I'm asking you, with what seems to be very good sense — apart from my private feelings, my very warm private feelings — to be my wife.'

★ ★ ★

She had never felt so dreadful in her life. His proposal had about it the fragility of fine glass, so quick and easy to break. She didn't know what to do. Everything in her cried out her need, her desire to accept his proposal, but now she couldn't. To tell him the truth would be disaster. To even accept his proposal would be disaster, because once he got a sight of her birth certificate, he would never trust her again.

There was nothing for it but to invent someone else she was interested in. She said, tight-lipped, 'Isn't it the limit? Nobody gets what they want! You think you want me, and I think I want . . . someone nearer my age, and all I get is Tom Kelford. Well, he doesn't mind anything except horses, and of course,' she finished, with a little twisted smile, 'horses are my thing. You really had forgotten that, Keith, my dear, hadn't you?' and she permitted herself to touch his face with one finger, a soft caressing movement in itself.

He just stared at her, then he caught and held her hand roughly to his face.

'You can't mean it!' he gasped. 'You're not turning me down? Oh, Rachel, you can't mean it!'

Her own eyes were brimming with tears. 'I'll never forgive myself for this,' she said thickly. Then she sat up abruptly, tearing her hand from his face. 'Oh, one of us has to have some sense, and it's got to be me. Keith, you can't marry me. You know you can't. I allow I might well make you comfortable within doors but you'd have to go out sooner or later. Think of the agony you'd suffer, having to face the district with a wife so much older than yourself! They'd talk about your marriage. There'd be publicity. There always is. No, it wouldn't do and I don't know why I let — ' She bit her lip to stop the flow of angry hurt words, and altered it to, 'I don't know why I came here in the first place.'

She couldn't bear to look at him, and as he wouldn't move, she had to be the one to get up, leave her couch and go out of the room. She ached in every bone in her body and had been glad to be lying there resting, but she had to go. If she didn't, she'd be throwing herself at him, she thought, and damning the consequences. It wasn't in reason, the way she wanted that young man.

He still sat there, staring at where she had been, and Rachel almost weakened and came back to him, unable to bear that hurt, lost look on his face. He hadn't told her everything that had happened at the hospital, she was sure. And now he wouldn't. He would suffer.

She was saved from going back, capitulating, by someone being admitted to the front door. It was the actress, Verena West.

Rachel couldn't escape in time. Verena had seen her. 'I know you!' she exclaimed at once. 'I ought to know you — but I can't think where I've seen you before. Don't tell me where, darling — let me work on it! I'll get it!' and on the same breath, she said, 'Where's Keith — I must see him at once, before the mood goes. Oh, it's a heavenly, heavenly house,' and she twirled round, her draperies flying. Verena usually wore soft draperies and impossible hats. Nobody ever forgot her, whatever she wore. Today she was anybody's beautiful sister, coming to call with all the devotion of family in her outspread arms. Rachel felt sick at such blatant acting.

Albert, doing door duty, murmured to Verena, 'It's Miss Beamish, the master's secretary, madam,' and he showed Verena into the second best salon. It was a cool, impersonal room in pale greens and greys and got the slanting late sunshine across one of the rose gardens. Verena frowned, intent now on trying to remember where she had seen that slight, grey-haired person before, and failed.

Rachel limped up to her room and lay on her bed, flat on her face. After last night's exhaustion, today had been just too much. She took off her glasses, buried her face in her pillow and cried as she hadn't cried for months. Her tears were not the relieving kind. She was crying because she had been forced to let slip through her fingers the one thing she wanted in all the world.

She went to sleep and didn't go down until it was almost time for dinner. She had no idea how Keith had received Verena. He had known she was due, but she supposed he had forgotten it. She thought with a little scared flutter, that she had done terrible things to him: both in refusing his quite sincere proposal of marriage and flinging him at once into Verena's path, without even the barrier of Melanie's caustic tongue nor the helping hands of Carol and Hazel — each with their own futures to look out for.

Rachel had to go downstairs sooner or later, so in one of the dark long-sleeved high-necked dresses that Keith, in lighter vein, sometimes referred to as her 'dear old aunt' clothes, she appeared at the door, looking and feeling far from well. Verena was in the middle of some dramatic pronouncement, and fully expected to keep Keith's attention but he leapt to his feet.

'Rachel! What have you been doing? You should have been resting!' and he shot across the room, his hands outstretched.

Verena murmured, laughter in her voice, 'I know resident secretaries in the backwoods are hard to find, Keith darling, but is this the way they have to be pampered, to keep them?'

Keith said, over his shoulder, 'Rachel was hurt in the stables' fire last night,' so Verena, quickly recovering, got up herself and fussed over Rachel, demanding to hear all about it, and sympathising which was infinitely worse.

Rachel said, with difficulty, 'I merely came to find out if Miss West is staying the night. I have to prepare her room if she is,' and to Verena, she explained, 'I am also the housekeeper.'

'Then of course I'm staying, dear, aren't I, Keith?' Verena returned gaily. 'And of course you mustn't stir yourself to do a thing about it. Let the maids do it. Goodness, if you've had an accident you should be in hospital! Well, why don't I take over? I'm 'resting' at the moment, Keith. I assure you, I am a very good secretary and housekeeper. Goodness, I've had to learn the parts — I know just what to do. Then that's settled.'

Keith said frigidly, 'I was going to have you settled in a very good hotel in Bexfield, Verena, for obvious reasons. I haven't had a chance to tell you but I'm caught up with an infectious case at the moment, at the hospital — some children on my estate here. I shall be out all day — using their lab if they'll let me. Mine isn't equipped for that sort of research.'

If he thought Verena was going to shrink from the idea of contagion, he didn't know how tenacious she could be. 'Then I'll stay here and run things and look after your perfect secretary for you.' And there was no dissuading her from that.

Short of being rude and asking her to go, Rachel thought, remembering other such occasions. Why had she done it? Mainly, she supposed, because she hadn't wanted, at the time, to be alone with Keith, after that dreadful scene earlier today.

Verena's personality, as Rachel knew well enough, was the same steam-roller kind as Melanie's, except that Verena covered it with convincingly gay laughter and deprecating shrugs and play of the hands.

At first, Keith didn't think she was so bad, but by the time she had 'arranged' everything to her satisfaction, with the all-male house staff eating out of her hands, Keith was tired of it, and Rachel wishing heartily that she had stayed in her room altogether. But it would have ended the same. From the moment Verena had said she was coming to see Keith, it was done. Verena had meant to stay in the house. She would have managed it somehow or another.

To Rachel's infinite relief, the vicar

and his wife came. Keith had apparently promised to revive the Bridge evenings his uncle had liked so much. Verena was pleased. Rachel escaped. She knew she wouldn't be able to bear watching Keith play that very bad game of his: why had he allowed himself to agree, she wondered. But of course, he would have been thinking of other things: the children, of course.

The vicar's wife came up to see Rachel later. 'What happened in the night, my dear? The doctor told us a very odd story. It didn't sound like Melanie at all, not to come and look for you.'

'I don't think she knew I was still out there,' Rachel said fairly, and gave a brief account of what had occurred.

'Oh, I see,' the vicar's wife said. She looked thoughtfully at Rachel, and murmured, 'You know, I don't think I've ever seen you without make-up before. Forgive me but you look very much younger.'

Rachel felt hunted. Sooner or later

she would have to give up this job, but until she did, she had the urge to have a woman friend, and she felt that this was a woman she could trust, so she said shortly, 'How young?'

The vicar's wife turned the bedside lamp on to Rachel's face. 'Twenty-two? Or less?' and she smiled.

Rachel put her hands up to her face. 'Oh, good heavens, what made me think that this could go on?' Through her hands, she said, 'I'm an actress — perhaps you know that. That's how Keith first met me. I'd been doing a middle-aged part and he . . . well, that's what he thought I was: middle-aged.'

'And you let him?' Mrs. Elmore asked gently.

'Of course. Oh, I can't explain but I've got myself into a corner through the most awful set of circumstances, and it's absolutely imperative that I keep my age a secret, especially from Keith. You won't let him know, will you?'

'Oh, dear, fancy me — the vicar's

wife — getting into this position,' Mrs. Elmore murmured, a half smile touching her lips. 'It really isn't any business of mine, I suppose, my dear, but couldn't you dye your hair and let him know, because I am sure you'll make him a very good wife. He always looks so comfortable when he's with you, I've always thought.'

'No. Circumstances!' Rachel said shortly. 'Family ones, mostly. I'm sorry I can't tell you, but I *mean* that, and I think I shall have to leave soon, just as soon as I get him married, and there are only twelve weeks left for that.'

'Yes, well,' Mrs. Elmore started to say, then broke off, listening. She went softly to the door and opened it, but came back frowning. 'Uncharitable of me, no doubt, but I thought I heard someone moving outside.' She studied Rachel worriedly. 'How will you get him married in time, my dear? Have you a plan?'

'Yes. I was lying here thinking about it when you came up,' Rachel said. 'I know someone who is rather nice. She doesn't like horses,' and they exchanged a brief conspiratorial smile. 'Nor the countryside, much, and she isn't in any way connected with laboratories or libraries. She's a great friend of mine and a very nice person. If I were to write a note to her, could you post it without anyone knowing?'

'I could indeed,' Mrs. Elmore said. 'Do I know her?'

'She's a singer,' Rachel said in a preoccupied voice, as she reached for her writing case and started to scribble a hasty note. 'Fern Farraker.'

'Fern Farraker! Oh, I *am* glad. She's a great favourite of the vicar's and mine. When we had a poor London parish she came and sang at one of our concerts, without a fee.'

'Yes, she would do that,' Rachel agreed warmly, and scribbled busily.

Mrs. Elmore badly wanted to know what was going into that letter. Like Rachel she had already formed an opinion that Keith wouldn't stand for plotting or dissembling in any way. Finally, she couldn't bear it, and murmured, 'How will you make such a visit look natural?'

Rachel looked up, smiling briefly. 'I'm not trying to. Fern doesn't like plotting either. No, it's a straight invitation for the children's talent contest. I've mentioned you, too. She won't be able to resist it. And if she helps, then Keith will ask her to stay overnight out of courtesy, I'm sure. She can take it from there, or just be a nuisance value. Verena won't like it, of course,' and they grinned at each other in happy conspiracy. 'Lucky she's in this country at the moment,' Rachel said as she licked down the envelope, and put a stamp on it. Passing it to the vicar's wife, she said, 'I *am* so glad you came up. I wanted someone to talk to.'

'About . . . everything?' the vicar's wife asked delicately. 'I must tell you I have a lively interest in other people's lives. I have to have, or I wouldn't be much good.'

'I might tell you everything, one day, but not now. I've got to think it all over first.'

'Well, without actually plotting, I'm very good at disentangling things,' Mrs. Elmore said with a smile, as she went downstairs.

Rachel lay back, rather more satisfied. This morning she had forgotten the children's talent contest. Now it was going to be the means of her great friend coming here. Fern would come, she knew.

* * *

Melmerstead had its share of things that had interested Keith's late uncle, and one of these was the Children's Home. Not all of the children were whole. There were those with legs in calipers, and those who couldn't walk at all, but all were either crippled or suffering some disability through being homeless, or suffering malnutrition or from cruelty. They came from Bexfield and the other five towns around Melmerstead, and because at the time of Keith's uncle's first quickening of interest in the home there had been at least five children who could sing or entertain in some way, he made it a chance of a career for them, and it was done through his annual talent contest. Other children competed, but almost always it was won by someone from the Home.

As Rachel had anticipated, Fern was most interested, and her coming made the affair such an occasion that the hall was crowded to suffocation. In Fern's wake came the press and television, and Keith found himself sponsoring yet another big social thing. But Rachel wouldn't go.

'It's because of . . . what happened, isn't it?' Keith murmured. He had searched for and found Rachel going to post a letter in the small box in the wall near the gates. Rachel had been walking fairly quickly, but when she heard his footsteps, she remembered to slow down and act her 'older woman's walk' and Keith was so anxious that he didn't notice then. He said, 'Rachel, won't you please re-consider? Tom Kelford isn't the chap for you . . . or were you having me on? I know — it's Shaw, isn't it? Why didn't I think of that before?'

Just for once they had both got away from Verena. Rachel stopped and looked up at Keith. His eyes seemed extra dark because they were in shadow, but that sensitive face of his was so unhappy, her heart ached for him.

'I'll make a bargain with you,' she said, 'but you must play fair, too. If at the end of the time, or almost at the end, if you still aren't married, I'll . . . well, I'll think about it. I'll do anything to help you because I know how much it means to you. But that's all I can say, and meantime you must play fair. You know what I mean.'

'Oh, Rachel,' he sighed and put his arm absently round her shoulders. His touch made her shrink away from him.

Never had she felt so shattered at any man's touch.

Keith looked hurt. 'You don't like me!' he accused.

'Oh, Keith, don't be damned silly,' she snapped. 'I'm bruised and aching all over — I would have admitted it before only I was afraid you'd banish me to bed. I'll go — when I get back. That's why I won't go to the concert.'

It was a matinee, because of the children. They were to come back to the house afterwards for a great tea of sickly buns and cakes and trifles and jellies. The excellent chef procured for Keith was thrilled about it, and beamed all over his face.

'Oh, I'm sorry you're not well, Rachel. How shall I manage the kids?' He pulled a face. 'Verena doesn't like children.'

'But your other celebrity does, I believe. She'll manage.'

'Well, let me post that. You get back to the house. You shouldn't be walking in that condition,' he insisted, so, as

Verena was calling them, Rachel was glad to go back alone, and finally Verena persuaded Keith to walk in the grounds and leave the letter for the staff to post.

She never left him alone with Rachel, Keith thought in irritation. He wondered how he'd manage tonight, and thought again about Rachel and how wonderful it would have been if she had been beside him and not Verena.

Hazel and Carol were both there at the Church Hall, he found later, with the same children both had entered in the gymkhana. He supposed gloomily that now that Melanie had been taken to France by the Colonel, for a sudden trip to buy horses, they now thought they had the field clear. He wondered how Verena would get on with them and what they would think of her.

Verena was resourceful. Keith found she had sent for both Simon and his fiancée Joan — both friends of hers and both eager to see her installed as Keith's wife. Joan would manage the children, too, together with the doting Simon.

Rachel wondered what would happen when they all came back to the house. She had said she felt too unwell to go and help but she wanted so badly to see the effect of Fern on Keith. As housekeeper she had prepared a room for Fern, and knew that Mrs. Elmore would be only too happy to see that nothing went wrong with their plan. But she didn't know that Joan and Simon had been sent for, nor did she know that Fern knew and liked them both.

She had been asleep when the mini-buses bringing the children arrived. The noise they made was like a lot of young starlings, drowning the sound of the voices of the grown-ups. Rachel stood on a chair to get a good view of them from her window, and her heart sank. Fern wasn't with them. But Neville Shaw was there.

Rachel fumed. What could have gone wrong? Fern had answered her letter to say she would come! If only she could get down to the library and telephone the Vicarage.

Everyone was in the sun room, and there was so much noise that Rachel was sure it would be all right. She couldn't wait to hear how things had gone.

She got through to the Vicarage and Mrs. Elmore answered.

'Oh, I wondered if it would be you, my dear,' she said. 'Have you heard what happened? No, I thought you might not — I heard you were keeping to your bed. Are you really in pain? Shall I come over?'

'I'm just bruised,' Rachel admitted. 'Didn't Fern come?'

'Oh, yes, and she carried the show,' Mrs. Elmore laughed. 'You want to talk to her?'

'Soon, but why didn't she come back here? She adores children.'

'She's staying with us. I thought I'd bring her over tomorrow. It went better than I've ever seen it before. Keith's uncle would be proud if he could have been here. Press, TV — the lot, because of Fern, of course.'

'I'm glad,' Rachel said fervently, but what she wanted to ask was how it was that Fern hadn't come back to show how well she could manage children, and how was it that she hadn't met Keith and been invited to stay. She was going to burst out with all that, when she remembered that this was only an extension. She said, 'Just a minute before you say any more — I'll be back in a minute,' with the intention of going to look out in the hall at the main telephone but at that moment there was a click, and when she had got to the door and looked out, the hall was empty. Who had it been, listening in? One of the staff? Or Verena? One of the staff, probably, Rachel thought with a sigh.

When she picked up the telephone again, Fern was on the line. 'Honey, what *is* going on?' the familiar deep throaty voice asked her, laughing.

'Too much to tell you over the telephone,' Rachel said.

'Oh, like that, is it? I did rather wonder,' Fern said with some amusement. Verena had never liked her, but Fern liked everyone and didn't understand the jealousies and other emotions in her profession. She lived to sing and to travel and nothing else much interested her, except children. 'There is an up-and-coming harpist in this little lot. Can you believe that?' she told Rachel. 'And a little girl with a clear golden soprano. I simply must try and get someone interested in her!'

Rachel said, 'Fern, I have to warn you — ' because she had remembered she hadn't told Keith that she knew Fern, but Fern had a warning to give, too. 'Rachel, you're going to get a visitor soon, one you won't like. You know that, don't you? I assure you, she's coming, and she means business.'

'Oh, no!' Rachel gasped, guessing who Fern meant. But at that moment the door opened and Keith looked in, so Rachel hastily said good-bye and rang off.

'Why, it *is* you downstairs, Rachel. Verena said she thought she heard you but I couldn't believe it.' He looked so absurdly pleased. 'Well, now you can come into the party, can't you?'

She shook her head. 'Please, no, Keith, I'm not cheerful enough or well enough.' And because he looked in perplexity at the telephone, she said hastily — 'Mrs. Elmore,' to explain the call. 'She's such a nice woman, isn't she?'

Keith's face cleared. 'Oh, so that's who you were talking to. I don't know who Verena thought you had on the line — she was very mysterious. Oh, I suppose Mrs. Elmore told you who was there. We had a celebrity.'

'Fern Farraker,' Rachel nodded. No point in hiding it now.

'I wanted to surprise you,' Keith said. 'Never mind. She won't have described her as I can,' and he took Rachel's hands in his. 'She's dark and beautiful

171

and happy, she loves children and she brings out the best in them. And she has a glorious voice like . . . ' and he broke off to try and think of a word, and finished with, 'Velvet. Is that a silly description?'

'Oh, I don't know,' Rachel said slowly. 'It's a very colourful description.'

'She's a colourful person,' Keith said, and although he was still holding Rachel's hands, it seemed an absent-minded gesture.

'You liked her,' Rachel said, feeling it was a wild understatement, and the knife turned in her heart as Keith said unexpectedly, 'She's a love of a woman!'

7

Verena was frankly glad to see the children go. They were a most unwelcome aspect. This young man, Keith, was boring enough in all conscience but she felt she could manage him, for the sake of the fortune he would acquire with this tatty old house. But it was disquieting to think that besides his unwholesome interest in that laboratory of his, he was also keen on the crippled little scraps of humanity she had seen performing so brilliantly today. She wasn't a born trouper like Fern, who adored whole-heartedly anyone connected with any form of the arts. Besides, Fern's generous nature made her find it easy to adore everyone. Verena had never liked Fern. An in-built jealousy against someone who had been endowed with a rich voice, good looks and an alluring personality that had made success come early, while she herself had pushed up the ladder the hard way and wasn't even past the half way mark, made her hate people like Fern.

Now she had another problem. It wasn't difficult to see that under Keith's perfect host manner, he expected her to depart with Simon and Joan. There was something in connection with that grey-haired secretary of his.

It was the gnawing anxiety to know more about that person that made Verena say, as they got out records to test the Hi-Fi system that Keith hadn't touched since his uncle's death, 'What about this secretary of yours? Does she like music? Why don't we have her down?'

It was the sort of remark that got instant response from Keith. Rachel had slid out of his persuasions to take dinner with them and had had a tray in the housekeeper's room and then she had escaped to bed. He said, 'What a good idea. I'll go up — '

'Good heavens, don't do that. You'll have the staff gossiping about her,' Verena put in quickly, with unerring shrewdness. 'No, I'll go up. Tell me where to find her. I'd like a word with her. I believe I've met her before. It's coming back to me.'

Joan, whose frankness had got her into hot water before, said blankly, 'But you *know* where you saw her before! As one of your own extras. We told you that, Verena!'

'No, I mean before that night!' Verena said hastily, and left them with Keith's instructions about how to reach Rachel's room.

Verena wasn't one to knock and wait for an answer. She tapped at Rachel's door and cried, 'Hello, it's only me!' and went in, without waiting for an invitation. Rachel had her glasses off, a bath cap covering the grey hair, and very little else on. Irritated she pulled her bath robe hastily round her and said, 'Don't you ever knock?'

Verena shut the door and said, 'Oh,

yes, the last time you said that to me, we had a little unpleasantness, if I remember rightly. Yes, I *thought* it was you. What happened to Peter?'

Rachel sighed and sat on the edge of the bed. How had she thought she could go through with this outrageous scheme? And all because she had fallen helplessly in love with Keith Chilton that first time she had seen him at the theatre. She said, 'He was just a silly boy, that Peter. He bored me. He should have stuck with you.'

'But you couldn't let him. You had to take him from me!'

'In point of fact, I didn't, but I suppose you'll keep on saying I did. I seem to have a flair for having young boys falling in love with me and it isn't what I want at all,' Rachel sighed.

'Any use asking what you do want?' Verena demanded nastily.

Rachel smiled ruefully. 'I used to think I wanted to act, but now I've gone right off it. Oh, help, now my head aches. I say, I do wish you'd go.'

'Not before you tell me what deep game you're playing.'

'Well, considering I made it easy for you to stay here by suggesting it to Keith,' Rachel began, but Verena cut across her.

'That is the one thing I don't understand and which I distrust very much. You wouldn't lift a finger to help me.'

'No, I don't think I would,' Rachel said frankly. 'We haven't exactly been friends.'

'Then why did you make it easy for me to get invited to stay here?' Verena insisted.

Rachel shrugged. 'To get Keith off the hook of a horse-loving girl who had practically caught him, with the help of her father.'

Verena said sceptically, 'No, that won't do. We've all heard, *ad nauseam*, the way he went mad because that girl left you in the burning stables and he rescued you. You want Keith for yourself!'

'What did you come up for, Verena?' Rachel asked tiredly, getting up. 'I was just taking a bath before crawling between the sheets to forget my aches and pains. My headache's getting worse.'

'Well, we can't have that, can we?' Verena sneered. 'Actually I came up to verify something. That I did know you. Now I've done that, I can tell you that if you don't have a bit of sense where Keith and his money are concerned, I shall see to it that he knows what I know about you. Yes, you know that would be fatal, don't you?' and nodding with satisfaction, she swept out of the room.

But as she went downstairs, she was simmering with fury. How stupid men were! She doubted whether Keith would believe her if she did tell him what she knew about Rachel. He might already suspect Rachel wasn't the middle-aged person he had been told she was, but she had had the wit to dye that hair of hers instead of wearing a grey wig, and to Keith that would suggest someone quite different from the person he would hear about from Verena. No, he'd never believe it. But she'd have to make him. Rachel must go, if she herself was to be in charge here. And how could she accomplish that, in the few hours left as a guest in this house? Keith had made it so clear that there was no reason for her to stay, that already Simon and Joan were talking of taking her back with them tomorrow. Keith and his recommending a good local hotel for her, indeed! He really was an anti-social animal. And Fern was still staying at the Vicarage.

It was the thought of Fern comfortably ensconced so near and she herself being swept away by her friends, that nagged at Verena and took her mind off the narrow stairs down from Rachel's room. She slipped.

Her heels weren't the highest she possessed, and she soon recovered her balance, and Rachel, with the bath water running, didn't hear the scuffle.

Verena thought about it, and went down to her room to change her shoes into really high-heeled ones, and went back to Rachel's steep stairs. There she staged another fall, this time screaming. Keith and the others heard it downstairs, but Ben — already doing his evening duties of turning down the beds and putting in hot bottles — got there first and carried her down.

Keith felt a sinking of the heart. He didn't want Verena here any longer. It was odd. Rachel herself had suggested that Verena should stay yet it was clear she didn't like her. He had wanted the house to himself, to have out with Rachel a scheme to end this wretched business of finding a wife for him. It was now no longer the need to inherit. It went deeper than that and he didn't know how. He didn't understand any of it. He just knew he didn't want Verena there.

The swelling of Verena's ankle necessitated the calling in of the local G.P., who was quite casual but definite in his assertion that Verena couldn't be moved for at least a week. Keith's spirits sank.

He didn't notice the glint of triumph in Verena's eyes. She had 'turned' her ankle many times in the past, learning what all actresses have to learn — how to fall down a flight of stairs without injury. And never before had anyone bothered about a slight swelling or made her rest up for a week like this stupid country G.P. It was a pity they hadn't, she thought, in satisfaction. She accepted the commiserations of Simon and Joan, and congratulated herself on the fact that that too-clever Rachel could do nothing about it. Verena was here to stay.

Rachel didn't hear about it until Joan went up later to bid her goodbye. 'You're going tonight?' Rachel cried. 'But I thought you'd stay here and go easily in the morning!'

'No point now. Verena's hurt her ankle falling down your stairs — didn't you hear the fuss? I confess I thought it was 'rigged' at first,' Joan admitted, in all honestly, 'but Keith was worried, poor lamb — he doesn't suspect guile in anyone — and he called in the doctor, who confirmed that Verena's got to rest for at least a week. So we're returning to London.'

Rachel murmured to herself, 'What have I done?' and looked frankly bothered. Joan, who felt the urge to be friends with Rachel as everyone did, said, with a half smile, 'Am I supposed to pretend I didn't hear that or to ask what you mean by it?'

Rachel shrugged, and pulled off the bath cap, then remembering something, hastily put it on again. Joan leaned forward and pushed it back, her sharp eyes having taken in what Rachel was trying to hide — the line where the hair sprang healthily away from the scalp. 'Oh. I see. You'll have to do something about that, won't you? So that explains the grey Alice Band at the hair-line! I wondered!'

She sat back and regarded the

scowling Rachel who had put on her glasses again. 'I think it was ambitious of you,' Joan remarked, 'and given luck you might have carried it through, but you know, Keith isn't like other young men. He can't have a good laugh at himself, I should think. He won't forgive being made a fool of.'

'I didn't mean to,' Rachel said, in an upset voice. 'At first it was an escape for me, when he offered me this job. I really wanted it. Then when I got to know him I sort of got protective about him and thought I'd try and find him someone he could bear to be married to. It's not his 'thing', marriage, you know. He really doesn't want marriage. He just wants his lab, his work, the kids and to find a cure for that disease. If he ever does find it, I don't know what he'll do then. Probably return to work in some hospital. He hates it here.' She examined her hands, and Joan noticed for the first time that they weren't white and soft like Verena's, but hard-working hands, like a nurse's, she thought. But

Rachel belonged to the world of theatre, she knew.

While she was puzzling over that, Rachel went on, 'You won't like this, because Verena's your friend — '

But Joan, honest as always, was impelled to say, 'Yes, but I don't always agree with her, and after these last few days, I don't think Keith would be happy with her, if that's in your mind.'

'Well, I did push him, in a way, to have her to stay,' Rachel admitted, 'but only because he was getting in a tight spot with the three local girls — the horsey ones. You know — Melanie and Hazel, oh, and that Carol creature. I couldn't stand her, and when Keith let himself be swayed by Neville's warning that her grandmother had been a great friend of Keith's uncle, I thought I ought to do something to stop it. Only then I got in a tight corner.'

Joan sat still and said nothing. Blunt as she was, she knew when to be silent. She had just remembered how she had seen Rachel once, before she had dyed

184

her hair. Rachel had just come from her own home, and there was such a deep-seated unhappiness in that girl's eyes, that Joan had felt wretched herself for the rest of the day, especially as Rachel must have realised suddenly what she was betraying in that face of hers, and promptly slid into acting jolly, which made Joan more miserable. Rachel, as herself, was not beautiful so much as striking. She could alter her face as much by acting as by make-up and Joan wondered miserably what would happen when Keith found out. 'Well,' she said, 'my friend Verena is here. In possession — on the spot. And I understand time is running out. What will you do?'

'I'll think of something,' Rachel said fiercely. Fern was the answer, of course. Rachel remembered, with pain, the way Keith had spoken of her. Well, better Fern married to Keith. Fern was kind and generous. Come to think of it, it might work out very well, because Fern wouldn't want to give up her singing, her concert tours, her world-wide travel — and that would leave Keith for long periods in the sanctuary of his lab.

That thought gave her peace of mind to sleep on it, but it didn't help next day. Verena was impossible. 'I want you to wait on me, dear,' she whispered with a half smile, 'you, and nobody else!'

'Oh, don't be ridiculous,' Rachel snapped. 'I've got mountains of work to do. And don't hold threats over my head, either.' But of course, Verena's threat was a very real one, so Rachel managed to combine everything, going back to work at her desk, and succumbing to answering Verena's bell ringing until Keith accidentally heard what was going on, and interfered, much to Rachel's surprise.

'Rachel was injured, too, you know,' he told Verena, in a puzzled voice. He looked less friendly in his white coat, fresh up from the lab for his favourite mid-morning coffee and fruit cake with Rachel. He had forgotten Verena's presence, and betrayed the chagrin he felt. But when Verena said sweetly, 'You'd forgotten me, hadn't you?' characteristically he felt he should make it up to her so he suggested that Rachel should have her mid-morning drink with them where Verena was resting on the sun room lounger. He was very much put out when Rachel curtly refused. But at least Keith stopped Verena from running Rachel about, and while Keith was taking his coffee with Verena, Rachel took the chance of an uninterrupted telephone call to the Vicarage, which resulted in Fern coming over for lunch.

'You didn't mind, did you?' Rachel asked Keith. 'She's a good friend of mine. I suppose I should have asked you first, then I remembered that she and Verena don't get on.' And she watched Keith's face light up in anticipation.

Fern's visit lightened the atmosphere considerably. 'But what on earth do you think you're going to do, love, to get out of this impasse?' Fern asked her softly, at Rachel's bedroom window, as they watched Verena being carried out to the swinging hammock in one of the sunken gardens, Keith in dutiful attendance.

'Well, I had several good ideas but I couldn't do them alone,' and she looked hopefully at Fern.

'Now you know I won't plot, not even for you!' Fern scolded.

'No,' Rachel sighed. 'But Verena's blackmailing me. She's going to tell him who I am, if I don't do what she wants.'

Fern stared. 'That should be no problem, considering his cousin is coming here anyway. She'll tell him, so why mind about Verena?'

'His cousin won't tell him. She won't get a chance of seeing me,' Rachel said, tight-lipped. 'She's just coming here to badger him about contesting the Will or sharing the money, with a hard luck tale. Or she might be going to descend to a form of blackmail, too. I wonder she hasn't before. After all, my dear cousin Charlie must surely be in trouble again because of being broke. And my brother Tim must surely be having a smack at borrowing a bit of cash from his employers. Any little thing like that would be enough to worry poor Keith into taking a dive into marriage to get at money to put an end to his cousin's wailing. He's terrified of her. And anyway, this Will permits of no breath of scandal, and he does need that money to keep up this house, and he needs the house because his lab is set up here. It's a vicious circle,' she said, kicking the leg of the table.

'I was thinking,' Fern said delicately. 'Why don't you marry him yourself? Well, the way he talks about you — '

'Have a bit of sense, Fern. The details on the marriage lines — remember? I'd never get away with it . . . even if I wanted to,' she added hastily. 'As a matter of fact, I've been pushed into such a corner with my stupid plotting that I've had to tell him there's someone else in my life.'

'Oh, it isn't true about his solicitor, then? He was telling Joan.'

'No. It's . . . ' Rachel drew a despairing breath and said, 'Tom Kelford, another local horse lover. Keith hates him.'

Fern said faintly, 'Oh, no! He won't like that! Poor Keith.'

But the atmosphere was considerably lightened by Fern being in the house. In the evening she sang for them. Verena insisted on sitting at the piano and accompanying her. She couldn't bear to be out of the limelight altogether. They had a fascinating time taping Fern's voice, too, on the extra equipment that Keith's late uncle had installed. Verena insisted on being taped, too, but it was worth it to keep her sweet until that ankle of hers healed. She was so anxious to tape a special part she had dreamed of getting in a new play that was being cast in London.

Keith good-naturedly let her. She was good in the part, he had to admit. But

Verena could never do a simple or natural thing. She had to be devious. 'I can't do it alone. There has to be this young girl to feed me with my lines,' she complained.

'Will I do?' Fern asked quickly, following the trend of Verena's scheme.

'No, of course not,' Verena snapped. 'Your voice is much too deep and rich. No, it has to be a light-weight voice. Like your housekeeper's voice, Keith. Where *is* Rachel?'

They called her, but Rachel had missed the earlier working up to this point, and didn't understand Fern's warning shake of the head, as Rachel good-naturedly agreed with Verena that she would be the 'feed'.

Rachel saw the trap too late. Keith was sitting at the back of them all, working the equipment. Something was going on between the three women and he didn't know what it was. Verena said suddenly, 'I can't get the feel of the thing — it's your hair, I suppose. Look — go up to my room. There's a case of props. Get a wig and put it on, to suggest a young girl. That'll give me atmosphere. Go on — a brown wig. No, a red one.'

Rachel was so caught out, she couldn't help the way she looked. It was the look of a person betrayed.

Fern said 'No!' at the same time that Keith said it. They all looked round at him in sheer surprise. He looked really angry for such a mild quiet young man, and into the silent atmosphere his words dripped ice as he said, 'For your information, Verena, I don't care for red-headed people, so don't mention such a thing again. Now if you insist on doing this part with my secretary's help, let's get on with it, but speaking personally, I have rather lost the taste for the exercise.'

Verena said surprisingly, 'Yes, all right. I didn't know how you felt. Let's forget about it. It was rather weak of me, wishful thinking and all that. I'll never get that part,' she finished with a deep sigh. 'I'd do much better not to keep dwelling on it by having my voice taped reading the lines. Thanks a lot, everybody, anyway, for being patient with me.'

Keith looked pleased, which infuriated Rachel. Oh, that Verena would have him in the hollow of her hand with her acting, if Rachel wasn't careful. She must be chased out of this house, to let Fern have her chance with Keith. Rachel was pretty sure that Fern was beginning to like him rather a lot.

Plotting at all wasn't easy, not only because of Verena's now limping about and being everywhere when a private telephone call needed to be made, or a conversation conducted, and added to Verena's presence was the string of visits on the part of Tom Kelford.

'Why can't you take my word for it that I'm a working woman?' Rachel stormed at him one day when she met him at the end of the drive.

'Because you fascinate me,' he said cheerfully. 'You wear oldies and act like my aunt when everyone's looking, but

193

when you wanted to catch your male first floor maid yesterday in the village I saw you run, and no aunt of mine ran like that, and no aunt of mine turns her head quickly like you do, which,' he said, running his finger down her carefully made-up throat, 'makes me wonder what stage make-up is doing on a young firm throat like this and also makes me wonder whether I should be doing your boss a kindness to recommend him to a good optician. On seconds thoughts I don't think I will, though. Don't want him getting ideas about you, do we?' and he tried to lift the edge of the grey Alice band.

Rachel jerked her head back. 'All right. If you must know my age — I am a good six years younger than you are, Tom Kelford, and I've done worse things than this in the past to get a resident job I wanted, when I hadn't a hope of a good stage part. Also in case you didn't know it, my boss is terrified of young women. What are you going to do about it?'

They had left the road to take the short cut through the spinney to the street behind the village post office. At this time of day, nobody was in the spinney. Tom said coolly, 'This,' and the friendly arm that had been round Rachel's shoulders spun her round to him and he held her in a vice-like grip while he kissed her. Tom was as expert with girls as he was with horses, but he had never met anyone like Rachel before. Her lips promised so much but withheld so much. He let her go at last with a frown of uncertainty, aware that he wanted her more than he had ever wanted a girl before.

Rachel's mouth turned up at the corners, with wry silent laughter. She understood his dilemma. 'What are you going to do about it, Tom, dear? You are too astute, I imagine, to think you can take me dancing and stop on the way home for a quick cuddle — '

'All right, I know people talk about me and I know what they say!' he said savagely. 'I shouldn't treat *you* like that.

195

You must know better than that.'

'I'm not sure,' she said slowly. 'You're such an optimist and so self-confident. But then so am I, and I have to tell you that nothing short of marriage into a well-breeched local family will do for me. I'm alone and have a way to kick for myself, so watch it, Tom!'

'What's the matter with my family?' he asked indignantly, striding beside her in a fine rage, which was only part indignation, part uncertainty because he liked fun with girls, and the thought of a bachelor existence. 'Haven't they got enough cash to suit you?'

'Careful, Tom. I might begin to think things if you talk like that. Besides, what if your family *are* considered far from hard up? How much of it belongs to you, I should like to know?'

Normally, when a girl put that question to him, he kissed her until she forgot she hadn't had the answer, or he slick-talked her out of wanting an answer. Today, with Rachel, who could nettle him so much but leave him vaguely wanting heaven knew what, he found himself saying frankly, 'Plenty, as it happens. There's a fat legacy waiting for me if I do marry someone an old aunt approves of. That shook you, didn't it?'

Rachel was shaken. Not by that information, but by what she was doing. Literally forcing Tom into a corner to propose marriage to her. But it was necessary, vitally necessary. Sooner or later she must show Keith she had meant what she said about being interested in someone else. Sooner or later Verena would go back on her word and make sure that Keith found out who Rachel was, or at least found out that she had deceived him about her age and made a fool of him into the bargain.

Somehow she must get rid of Verena. She walked soberly beside the now enthusiastic Tom, who had remembered that he had seen Rachel riding, on that one occasion early that morning with Keith, and that she had an excellent seat. He told her so. 'Well, what are you scowling for? Lots of girls bumping up and down on hacks in this district would love to be told that!' and he never realised how Rachel hated him in that moment, for having seen her that time with Keith, in what she now treasured as a memory. An early morning dew-spangled memory of an event that could never happen again.

With her heart crying within her, she marched forward, and going into the Sub-Post Office she heard someone talking about the performance the cripple children had given at the show when they had found the harpist and the little girl with the golden voice.

She caught her breath. The cripple children! Her way out, she thought, as she mentally burnt the last of her boats and said goodbye to her future happiness.

8

Keith nervously watched the calendar. The weather had turned sharp and cold again, but two days later a heatwave returned, making the lab a frustrating place to work in. He had been to the hospital to see the children from Pond Cottage and he was feeling wretched. Dr. Henty, at the hospital, had diagnosed it as fever from the proximity of the pond. There was feeling there. Dr. Henty had been Medical Officer of Health at the time of Keith's uncle's row with the local people about draining the pond. It was a beauty spot, the cottagers didn't have to live there, having been offered adequate accommodation elsewhere on the estate and Dr. Henty had lost his fight. Now he wasn't likely to let Keith get his foot into the matter, since everyone knew how Keith was chasing this particular bug. Dr. Henty put the children into isolation and Keith couldn't get near them.

He told Verena. She would be there, looking all receptive, he thought, as he talked to her on the telephone. But Verena wasn't receptive. She was furious.

'She's done it on purpose!' she stormed. 'She knows what bad headaches I get and she's done it purposely.'

'Who, Verena? And done what?' he asked patiently.

Verena held the telephone away towards the open door and then put it to her ear again. 'Did you hear all that noise, Keith?'

'Well, yes, but what is it?' All he could think of was that Fern was the offender and had put on a tape of off noises to some show. He was well aware that there was no love lost between Fern and Verena. 'I'll be back in ten minutes,' he said, making up his mind. 'Now just go out and lie in the hammock under the tree where it's peaceful, and I'll see what's going on.'

But when he arrived, Verena wasn't in the hammock. She was in the garden room with the shades down, and cotton wool in her ears. And now he could hear what the noise was. Children's voices, many voices.

'Where's Fern?' he asked blankly.

'Gone into the town shopping,' Verena said in a surly voice. 'Ben drove her in the second car.'

'Well, what's happening? Oh, never mind, I'll see Rachel about it,' he said impatiently, hurrying away.

'*She* dreamed this one up — that Rachel!' Verena called out nastily. 'Keith, don't go — I've something to tell you!'

Keith was now too intrigued to stay with her. He found the noise by the process of elimination. There were thumps and shrieks of laughter in almost every room, and as he opened doors one by one, he found children with crutches, arms in slings, arms in raised plaster, not one of them whole,

201

but all of them looking extremely happy and having fun. 'Don't let her find us — shut the door!' they yelled.

Finally he tracked Rachel down, under the bear-skin rug, children riding her, whacking her and yelling.

'*Rachel*!' he roared, above the noise.

She got up, her glasses falling off, the bear-skin over one eye in a way that made her look decidedly tipsy. The children fell off, squealing with excitement, and scrambled to their feet, clutching her where they could, and laughing. 'We're here to stay,' they chanted. 'For as long as we like! *She* said we could!'

Rachel got quietly to her feet, and put her glasses back and nervously felt her hair to see if it was tidy. She had dispensed with the headband, having been to the hairdresser's for a touching-up. She said, 'I did have the permission of the Matron of the Home and I didn't think you'd mind.'

'Yes, but — why didn't you ask me first?'

She sorted around in her mind for a polite way to put it, then threw caution to the winds. She no longer cared. She was leaving soon, anyway. She would have to. 'If you want to know, I thought it might get rid of another guest,' and her face puckered into a grin of pure malice which his own face wanted to echo, but as host he dare not let it.

'Oh, I say, you really are the limit,' he said, stifling his laughter.

'Besides, the children are enjoying it here,' she added firmly. There was a skinny boy with one leg in irons, trying to climb up her back, so she absently put her hands behind her and gave him a bunk-up until he rode pick-a-back.

'Now do get down, Lenny,' Keith said. 'Rachel's not strong enough to — '

'Leave him!' Rachel said sharply. 'I love it.'

There was a silence. Keith was thinking confusedly that for a grey-haired little lady she was exhibiting a great deal of energy and pulling about. Verena, however, wasn't going to allow any cosy talks between them. She hobbled out, dragging her injured foot and holding on to the lintel of the door.

'Well, if you can't keep order in your own house, Keith — ' she began.

The children suddenly went quiet. One little boy poked a head round each of the three doors where noise was going on, and it stopped. They all stood and stared in hostile fashion at Verena.

'Well, what are those children staring at, for heaven's sake?' Verena snapped.

The children clung to Rachel, silent still, and one child with a sticky face absently put its lolly-pop against her cheek. Keith took out a clean handkerchief and began to wipe it, but Verena had to intervene. She couldn't bear the sight of Keith touching that girl.

'Oh, for heaven's sake,' she snapped, 'there's a wet flannel in the downstairs cloakroom. Come on, I'll help you get them cleaned up, Rachel, and you look as if a wash wouldn't do you any harm!'

The children huddled closer to Rachel. She had got a dozen of them over, he saw, at a swift count. 'I'll help you, Rachel,' Keith said, and lifted the boy off her back, but another little girl was up in no time. They just had to cling to Rachel, touch her, look at her, he saw; and they only transferred their attentions to someone else when Fern appeared at the front door, laden with parcels.

'Presents!' she called, and they rushed to her, but they dragged Rachel too. Keith went with them and Verena found herself alone.

Anger ate into her. This was her own bright plan recoiling on her own head, with a vengeance, and Keith didn't help by calling back to her, 'Go and rest, Verena. Now Fern's back, we'll see to this lot. Don't you worry.'

Verena returned to her couch, first ringing for the staff to take over the chores. Keith and Rachel would have no cosy opening of parcels or splashings with soap in the bathrooms, if she could help it.

'They'll have to go,' she insisted to

Keith later. 'You can't put that lot up here, and besides, don't they need special treatment?'

'Oh, we've plenty of room here, and besides, Rachel's sent for a couple of the nurses from the Home so the children can stay overnight. It's a great thrill for them. She's planned musical chairs and other parlour games for them. She's a wonderful person. As for Fern, she's as good as Rachel, in handling the children. For such a glamorous person, Fern is really surprising.'

'I bet she is,' Verena said bitterly.

Keith looked perplexed. 'It's that ankle of yours bothering you. I really am a thoughtless brute. I keep forgetting it. You must go up to your room. Yes, I insist! As far away from the noise as possible.'

The noise lasted all evening, and Verena grimly endured it because she couldn't bear to be out of things, wondering what Keith was doing with Rachel or Fern. Those two were friends, and no friends of hers, and somehow the value of her self-imposed accident had dwindled away.

The vicar's wife came over. Verena had no facts but guessed that Rachel had sent for her. The vicar's wife adored children. That evening they gave up to the children doing their party pieces for 'prizes' — things that Fern had brought back from the shops.

Worried, Verena saw that Rachel had pulled a fast one on her. As a stage actress it wasn't in reason that Verena shouldn't be interested in these children, unless she loathed young people. Verena dare not let Keith think that. So she forced her face into a bright smile, and played the piano for them when they needed accompaniments and did the same for Fern to sing the children's favourite songs.

'I *have* enjoyed this evening so much,' Keith said, looking at Fern but putting a friendly hand on Rachel's shoulder as he spoke.

She tried to slide away from his touch

but he held her shoulder firmly, and she couldn't bear it. It wasn't right that this man, who had no forceful personality with women, and was known to be reticent, keen only on his work, should be able to arouse such emotions in her. Fern watched her thoughtfully, and the vicar's wife enjoyed herself so much observing the whole lot of them. She decided she really must warn Rachel that Verena was not going to be a placid person to have around — she would make a bad enemy.

The nurses put the children to bed with the help of Rachel and the vicar's wife, but Fern, prodded by Rachel, stayed with Verena and Keith. Most of these children didn't remember what living in a house was like, and certainly none of them had ever been in a house like this.

Rachel prayed that Fern would make the most of this opportunity and only relaxed when she heard Fern start to sing.

Keith had asked her to. He was

fascinated by her voice. He sat watching the play of emotions on that beautiful face, the way the liquid dark eyes looked meltingly or angrily or like those of a woman in love, according to what she was singing. So different from the eyes of Verena, which were shallow, and, Keith considered, just the sort of eyes he would have expected an actress to have. And then he started thinking of Rachel again and his attention wandered. Rachel and those children . . .

Suddenly he excused himself, leaving the two women to their music, and went to find Rachel.

As he had anticipated, she was telling a story to the bigger children. A gory one, he thought, with a grin, as he caught the closing lines: 'And the prince, being a man to do his homework, clouted the wicked duke with his cudgel in the one hand and thrust home his trusty sword in the other, and if you think, kids, that a sword and a cudgel are a sissy compared with a laser gun in that sci-fiction I know you read, you just want to be on the receiving end of them and you'd know different.'

A delighted roar went up. But the girls wanted the love stuff. 'Did he marry the princess, Rachel?' they begged. 'Because he did love her or he wouldn't have risked his life for her, would he?'

Rachel and the girls ignored the boys' rude comments, while she gave it thought. Rachel finally played safe. 'Of course he loved her or he'd have stayed home and sent his soldiers out to fight, wouldn't he? It stands to reason!'

'But how did she know he was the one she loved? And how did she make him love her?' the little girl with the golden voice wanted to know. She could be rather awkward at times, Keith had noticed. A sweet little brat, but a bit of an exhibitionist. Rachel was equal to it, however.

'Well, I must tell you, Mandy, that when you're grown-up like the princess, you get a sort of magic happen to you,

210

just as if some one waved a wand over you, because I can assure you, you know all right, that you're in love, and who it is you love, and you get a sort of glow over you, that no one else can see except the man you love. You remember that! It's gospel truth.'

Rachel was a great success, especially as she went round to each faithfully and kissed the whole lot of them. Keith, hiding on the landing chafed with impatience in case Verena or Fern interrupted and spoilt it all.

At last Rachel came out, and jumped in sheer surprise. He was the last person she had expected to run into, out on that landing.

'Sh-h, don't make a sound,' he hastily cautioned her. 'Come into the music room. Want to ask you something, terribly important.'

Rachel was a sucker for the word 'important', Keith had discovered, but this time she was suspicious. He got her no further than the oriel window embrasure on the second landing.

'Rachel, I wanted to know about the kids. They love it here, and I love having them, but they'll have to go back tomorrow, you know, or Verena will do something to spoil it for them.'

Rachel's eyes narrowed. 'But the whole idea is to keep the kids here to drive Verena away. It will, too. Don't you want that?'

'Oh, do I not! But if you're sure — ? Funny, I thought you liked them here for themselves, Rachel.'

'Well, of course I do,' she snapped. 'Don't be more silly than usual, Keith, for goodness' sake.'

He was equal to that. 'You forgot to say 'sir',' he grinned. And as her face broke into an unwilling answering grin, he pressed home his small advantage, and said, 'How will you know you're in love, Rachel? No, don't try to escape. I have been told repeatedly that you're years older than I am — heaven knows how often you've told me so. But the human heart's a damned funny thing and I've been coming to the conclusion for ages that it's you, and only you. Surely I don't have to marry someone I shan't be comfortable with, just because of what other people think of the disparity in ages?'

His voice had roughened with emotion. Although his face was in shadow it wasn't difficult to know that it was embarrassingly filled with those inner thoughts of his that he usually kept decently hidden, and what it must have cost him to make that little speech only Rachel could know.

Rachel's turbulent thoughts screamed back at her: 'Do I have to say no to him? Am I sure he won't forgive me when he finds out who I am?' but at that moment Verena limped out into the hall and called up the stairwell to them.

'Keith, for goodness' sake what are you doing up there? I can see you! Who's with you? Come down, and finish what we were doing!'

Keith looked over the banister, and back at Rachel, but Rachel had taken the opportunity to slip away. It was all spoilt now, anyway.

★ ★ ★

To that end, Rachel agreed that the children should go back the next day. Why not? Keith wouldn't marry Verena, of that she could be sure. Verena had no heart for those children from the Home. That was the key.

But Fern had. She went with Keith and Rachel the next day to take the children back: Fern in one car, with Rachel driving, Keith driving one of the nurses, and the second nurse taking the batch of smaller children in her car. The kids had had a wonderful time but, as Keith had pointed out, it would be wicked to risk Verena spoiling their memory of their stay in the big house, as she might well do out of sheer spite.

Verena sat in the glass sun-room, reading the magazines, her leg up. Lying about had been fun at first, but now it was becoming boring. And then

214

she found a copy of a theatrical glossy magazine. In it was a notice that rehearsals for the one play she had always wanted to be in, were starting that day. In London and she was caught here, in this house, fighting a losing battle with Rachel and Fern. She put the magazines aside impatiently, to telephone about that part. She ought to have it. She was well-known enough. All of a sudden, the pale green telephone was beckoning with an insidious finger; the future she had wanted, dangling before her.

She leapt to her feet, but the foot she had been resting gave way and she was shocked to find herself flat on her face. With her heart beating painfully, she lay there a minute, thinking, then relief swamped her. Well, of course, what had she expected, after keeping that leg up for so long? It was bound to be a bit tricky at first!

She got herself up, carefully this time, and tried her foot on the ground. No pain, nothing. She sat down at the telephone and called the man she had been badgering for that part for so long. Every time there was a whisper that the play was going to be produced, she was hammering at poor Paul Doncaster's door, and every time it fell through, for lack of cash, her world crashed round her ears. Now, when she had persuaded Keith to marry her, she would have all the cash she needed, to be the play's biggest backer. So she would have the star part. Why hadn't she thought of that before?

'No, listen Paul,' she cajoled him, when he carefully explained that there wasn't even a certainty that he would have the cash to put it on. 'Paul, you *will* have the cash. All you want. *I'll* provide it. Of course I can, darling, aren't I trying to explain? I am about to marry someone with loads of cash, and in return for that teensy little part — don't you *see*, Paul?'

He listened to the excited throb of triumphant laughter at her end, and thought quickly while she talked hard.

Paul was hard-bitten and knew his Verena. She couldn't act, but if he got a good supporting cast and all the money she was insisting that she'd bring with her, it might be the answer to his own problems.

She put the telephone down at last, well-pleased. Now all she had to do was to bring Keith up to scratch and she thought she knew of a way. The two things went hand in hand together.

The door bell rang. She hadn't heard the sound of the taxi coming up the drive, she was so keen on marshalling her thoughts for that telephone call. Someone having difficulty getting past Ben, by the sound of it. A woman, with a voice that Verena thought she knew. She went out into the big entrance hall in time to see Ben almost managing to get rid of the caller.

'Who is it, Ben?' she asked. When she married Keith, she promised herself, Ben would go. He took too much on himself. Just the sort of servant you would expect that too-clever Rachel to have engaged.

Ben said, with a poker face, 'It's all right, madam, I'm seeing to this. Please don't worry, and mind that foot of yours.'

'Never mind my foot, Ben, and show the caller in! I'm alone and bored — go on, do as I say!' So Amelia Lawrence got past the front door.

Verena limped back into the small salon and ordered coffee and little cakes. 'You know, I'm sure I know you. Your face is familiar. Are you on the stage?'

Amelia stared. 'No, I'm cousin to the present owner of the house, Keith Chilton.'

'Oh. Then we shall be seeing a lot of each other, won't we, because Keith and I — oh, dear, I shouldn't have said that. Nothing is settled yet. But I'm so happy, I hardly know what I'm saying.'

Amelia smiled falsely, too. Both ladies disliked each other very much and because Amelia saw that here was the person who would thwart all her plans, she said gently, 'Oh, dear, I'm afraid you and Keith won't have much to live on, my dear, because as a scientist he's practically penniless. And when the Will is contested, well — perhaps I'm speaking too soon, but it was always to me that the house and the money was coming. Keith's uncle wasn't too — well, lucid, shall we say, at the least? Towards the end of his life, that is. But, of course, if you're on the stage, you will be well off enough to be able to keep my cousin Keith, won't you?' and she laughed, a tinkling little laugh that Verena echoed. 'But the Will will be contested, I assure you,' Amelia finished firmly, but with great good humour. 'Though I don't suppose you'll mind the publicity. Any publicity is good publicity, don't you stage folks say?'

Verena smiled thinly and ignored that. She said instead, 'I don't suppose you really believe you'll get far or what are you doing down here? Warning

Keith of a future legal battle?'

'Oh, no, I've come to see him about quite a different matter. My daughter Lydia — it's rather strange. She was supposed to be staying with another girl in a London flat, and she was missing, then there was a letter found, in which she said she was going away for a holiday. And now it appears she's been seen in *this* district. Well, of course, Keith must know — '

'Why?' Verena asked silkily. 'Why should Keith know anything about it?'

'He must do! Well, they were at the same hospital. She was a nurse, until she went on the stage. If she was in any trouble or hard-up, she might just come to Keith instead of to me and her stepfather, because she knew how we disapproved of her going on the stage. Of being a nurse, too. All the dreadful things those girls have to do!'

There was only one bit in all that which interested Verena and she pounced on it. 'On the stage? In what show?' she asked quickly.

'Oh, nothing grand,' Amelia said sweepingly. 'I don't know the names of the shows — she was what is called an extra, I believe, or is that a film term? Well, it wasn't even a speaking part — the idea of Lydia being either an actress or a nurse was quite absurd.'

'You carry a picture of her, of course,' Verena said, thinking.

'Naturally. I have several. This is the last one,' and Amelia got out a coloured picture from the depths of her huge leather bag.

Verena took it and studied it, her face going deadpan. 'Have you got any of your daughter in stage make-up?' she asked casually, and she felt she was choking with rage.

'No, but I have one of her with her best friend, Fern Farraker, the singer, you know. That girl will go far. Beautiful voice. A very nice girl, too. Good family. Now if Lydia had only a singing voice — but of course, she has nothing. Nothing at all. All she can do really well is to type. Oh, dear, how long is Keith going to be? I've telephoned and telephoned but he always manages to be busy and has to put the telephone down quickly.'

'Your daughter was an extra in the show I was in recently,' Verena said coolly. 'I remember distinctly because she made such a botch of her little part and the producer was livid. How astute you are, to see she just isn't for the stage!'

'You don't mean it!' Amelia didn't know whether to be relieved or indignant. 'But where is she now?'

'I've got a good idea. Now how about leaving it to me? If you were to go back to London and leave me to deal with Keith, I think I can put you on to your daughter pretty soon. Of course, until she's done something worthwhile you can't blame her for keeping out of your way, can you?'

It took a lot of persuasion to get Amelia into one of the house cars to be taken to the station, to await events in London. Keith could have told Verena that. But she went at last and Verena told Ben not to say she had called. 'It's a surprise,' she said firmly. And she settled back to await Keith's return with impatience.

Keith had taken Fern to lunch. Fern was a lovely person to be with. Rachel refused to join them. She had a distracted look and said there was something she had to do, and nothing could make her change her mind.

She looked back at them as she left them. Would Fern keep her promise? She had almost persuaded Fern to make Keith propose to her to save him from people like Verena.

'Think of it,' Rachel had urged. 'You keeping your concert tours schedule and leaving him in peace in his lab. Freedom for both of you, and he gets his inheritance. *Please*, Fern!' Rachel had pleaded. But whether Fern would do it was another thing.

Fern was very worried. It seemed absolutely sure in her eyes that Rachel was in love with Keith. She studied the young man. He was the quiet sort who just passes for a tall dark shy young man and that was the end of it. Now, looking at him really objectively, in the light of perhaps a future husband, she was rather surprised. There was a lot of character in that face. If he liked a person he let them see that rather curious sense of humour of his, and something was making him less shy and in-turning than he had been at first. She thought it was Rachel, and she would have loved to ask him, but Rachel hadn't admitted yet that Keith either knew or didn't know.

It struck her as strange that he couldn't tell that it was a young woman under all that make-up and grey hair, but then, of course, Rachel could act when she wanted to. Keith had already told Fern about how Rachel stopped the show by walking on, saying nothing, just being what she was supposed to be — a not-so-young secretary. He also added how annoyed Verena had looked for a moment until she recollected where she was. Yes, Rachel could act all right, and probably acted too well in this instance.

Now, looking at those sensitive eyes under the strongly marked brows, Fern was inclined to revise her first opinion of him. Here was a really good man, a man who would cherish a woman but who might be unforgiving if he felt he had been cheated or made a fool of.

So when, having with ceremony tasted the wine and ordered the meal, he turned to Fern and said suddenly, 'About this marriage of mine, Fern,' she wasn't ready.

He stared into her flustered face, with some consternation. 'Oh, my dear, I didn't mean to embarrass you,' he said kindly. 'I wanted your advice. About Rachel.'

That was a great deal worse. Fern said gently, 'You mean Verena, don't you?' but he shook his head, smiling and countered, 'No, I don't, and you know I don't. Fern, how could I marry someone like that? You know me — you must do by now, and you know what a farce it all is. If it weren't for my work, I wouldn't care so much about the old house, but there is, of course, the thought of pleasing my uncle. He was good to me. So ... I must choose someone, and the person I want, won't have me.'

Fern turned enquiring eyes up to his. He said, 'You're her friend. Has she not told you? You must know I'm talking about Rachel.'

'Rachel!' Fern nodded. 'Are you sure?' but of course, she could see he was sure. 'What is your problem, then, Keith?'

'We don't get very far when we discuss it, Rachel and I, though we are very close in discussions on almost every other subject. She tells me she's old enough to be my mother and I tell her that fellows marry regardless of age nowadays, and it gets to deadlock.'

'How old do you think she is, Keith?'

'I don't know,' he admitted. 'She puts on a lot of stage make-up and it makes her look frankly elderly and she stumps about as if she's long past her first youth which I feel instinctively is nonsense, because look at the way she allows the children to pull her about in play. Besides, I studied her riding performance one morning. She forgot I was so close behind her. Fern, Rachel is poetry on a horse's back. A person can't look fluid like that, as if horse and rider were one, and be middle-aged. All right, I didn't enjoy my ride, but I did enjoy watching her.'

'What happened then?' the intrigued Fern couldn't resist asking.

He laughed, gently reminiscing laughter. 'She lost her temper. She's got a devilish temper, you know,' he confided, as if it were some great gift. Proud of Rachel's temper, Fern thought tenderly. 'She rode off and left me,' he continued, 'and she hasn't been riding with me since. Doesn't like being watched from behind her.' He didn't give Fern a chance to gather her forces after that. 'How long have you known her?' he demanded.

'About fifteen years,' Fern said, not thinking. And when his eyebrows shot up in surprise, she said, 'I was seven when I met her — I'd just lost my parents and I hadn't been a boarder before, and Rachel was kind to me. Heaven knew she hadn't had much of a home life, but she always did like making other people stop being wretched.'

'Yes, she loves children,' he frowned, and Fern saw she was now embroiled in the tangle, because clearly he envisaged Rachel as an adult being kind to an orphaned unhappy child, when in fact they had been the same age.

She thought of Rachel, pulling faces to make her laugh, and sharing a bar of rather squashed chocolate. Telling Fern stories from a library book long overdue, and for good measure sharing a secret with Fern: some nonsense about the gym mistress being unsuccessfully in love with the new curate whose Adam's apple bobbed up and down. Rachel had literally badgered

Fern into forgetting her grief and learning to laugh again. 'She's my friend,' Fern said, not listening to him. 'And there's one thing I ought to do, if I am going to be a friend to her, only what can I do since she's forbidden me to do it?'

'Am I supposed to know what that means, Fern?' he bantered, but his eyes were serious.

Fern said, 'Well, I won't do what she forbade me to do. I'll just say this. I wish you'd settle for Rachel, no matter what. I'm sure it will turn out all right. I know what she feels about you, you see.'

★ ★ ★

Rachel had taken a taxi back to the house. She had remembered that Tom Kelford was expecting to see her. She didn't want him to come over, and Verena and Tom get together. Tom considered it a great joke that she had got away with pretending to be an elderly typist with grey hair. Rachel didn't trust him. He would most likely feel it was worthwhile keeping Verena entertained with such a story and then telling her not to pass it on. Tom was like that. He just didn't care. How was she going to feel, Rachel asked herself, if she married Tom?

It was not a question she could face just yet. Nor did she want to face Tom just yet. She decided to dismiss the taxi and go in by the french windows to the room where she worked, so that she could watch the drive for a sight of Tom's car before Verena could get to him. That leg of Verena's worried Rachel. Was it really the injury she insisted it was, or just a bit of acting to keep her at the house? But then, the doctor had insisted it was an injury and why would he say so if it wasn't?

She was restless and uneasy, filled with doubts and a vague unhappiness, her old sense of 'impending doom'. There was no car in the drive yet someone was coming out of the front door and she could hear Verena's voice. And Ben was gentling one of the house cars round to the front door to take the visitor away.

Rachel saw too late who the visitor was, and couldn't escape in time. Amelia Lawrence stood undecided, with Verena still talking behind her. As the door was being held open for her by Ben, resplendent in his uniform, Amelia shrugged a little, said goodbye to Verena and then got into the car. Rachel watched it vanish to the right at the end of the drive.

Rachel heaved a sigh of relief that she hadn't been involved in what might have been a difficult and embarrassing situation. But what on earth was Mrs. Lawrence doing visiting, with Verena? Rachel stood there thinking. Verena was on the telephone. She could hear her. Who on earth was Verena calling, just on the heels of Mrs. Lawrence's departure? Rachel had the uncomfortable feeling that it was about herself.

Logically, she thought, standing there

by her typewriter, she should go. Pack up and go while Keith was out with Fern. If only she could rely on Fern to stand up to Verena, not let Keith get into such a position that he had to marry Verena! Any of the others would have been preferable to the actress, Rachel thought bitterly. The others were at least countrywomen, and understood life that went on at the Grange. Verena was a Townie and would rip through Keith's money in no time. And it was all Rachel's fault: a little plot that hadn't come off.

There was a *ping* as Verena finished her telephone call, but almost at once it rang again, and Rachel picked it up. It was Amelia on the line, at the station. Rachel, who had spoken first, betrayed her voice and couldn't do a thing.

Amelia's voice came through sharply. 'It *is* you, Lydia, isn't it?'

9

Rachel sighed. 'Yes, it's me. Why don't you leave me alone, Mother?'

'Oh, you naughty girl, making me so worried!' Amelia scolded. 'When all the time you were doing something sensible. Before we say another word, go and see if anyone's on the extension. I wouldn't trust that Verena person not to listen in. Go on!'

'It's all right,' Rachel said impatiently. 'From where I'm standing, I can see it. Nobody's listening in. Anyway, it doesn't matter. I've made up my mind to leave here . . . today.' And that was an instant decision, the minute she had seen Amelia leave the house. There would be no peace now.

Amelia fairly danced with rage and frustration. 'Don't be an absolute idiot, Lydia! You're in a strong position to do something sensible for once. *I* recognised you, but I don't think anyone else would. Now all you have to do is to persuade that tiresome young man Keith to choose you as his wife, and we shall all be secure. Think of it, Lydia, just think.'

'I am thinking. I told you before, I won't marry money just to bale out the family. We've gone over it a thousand times. Now do go back home and leave me alone. I've lots to do. How did you recognise me, by the way?'

'I don't know. Something about the way you stand, or perhaps you forgot to act as an older woman. Does it matter? Anyway, if you don't get moving with that Keith, there's an actress called Verena West who very soon will! In fact, she's saying she's engaged now!'

'Then what are you worrying about?' Rachel retorted and hung up.

It was always the same. Her mother was so sure that all that had to happen was for Rachel to make a successful marriage, and all their troubles would be over. She wondered what would happen if she had told her mother that Keith would never marry her now, because she had deceived him.

She went up the back stairs to her room. Verena had had the door open a crack and had at least heard Rachel's half of the conversation and guessed the rest. She had had a bad moment when she realised Rachel hadn't stayed with the other two but she thought Fern wouldn't be too pushing. And now this had happened. She remembered Keith's antipathy towards red hair the night they had been about to tape her part in that play. What would he think now? Her lips curled into a smile of pure anticipation.

Keith and Fern came back at tea-time. Verena watched them narrowly and decided that Fern hadn't made any headway with Keith. She said happily to them both, 'I feel a lot better and I've been getting about on my bad ankle. And I've got some news for you, Keith dear.'

Fern looked at them both and got up

to go but Keith told her to stay. 'What news, Verena? You can speak before Fern.'

Verena kept her happy smile steady with an effort, and said, 'I've had a telephone call — from the man who's putting on that play. Paul Doncaster. And guess what? I've got the part of my life — the part I've always dreamed of!'

Keith said, in a little more heartfelt tone than was perhaps necessary, 'You can't think how glad I am about that, Verena. But are you sure you're quite fit for it? You ought to let our doctor clear you, you know.'

Verena laughed. 'Darling boy, do you think I'd take on anything so important to me without getting his clearance? It's all right, I tell you! In fact, I shall be driving up to London tonight. Rehearsals start tomorrow.'

'But you can't drive tonight — you must be mad!' Keith exploded.

'My car is auto drive, darling, remember?' Verena reminded him. She got up, carefully putting that foot to the ground as she talked, and much to her relief it didn't feel too bad. 'See? Of course, I could wish I had a companion — I suppose you wouldn't like to come with me, Fern? Just for the company.' She held her breath as she asked the question, confident that as Fern didn't like her she would refuse, and that Keith would offer to drive her up to London himself. All she wanted was a stretch of time without interruption, in which to pin him down to propose to her. But to her surprise and chagrin, the resourceful Fern said quickly, 'Yes, I'll be glad to come with you. I was thinking of returning to London anyway. It will suit me very well. By the way, is Rachel back yet?'

'Yes, but I think she went out,' Verena said impatiently, trying to cope with this new aspect.

Fern gave her little opportunity to re-marshal her thoughts. She said, 'I must talk to Rachel. I'll go and see if she's in her room,' and she hurried out, leaving Keith with Verena.

Now Verena, nettled, had to change her plans fast. She drew a deep breath and said, 'Don't go, Keith! There's something private and personal I wanted to say. I thought Fern would never go!'

Keith had his 'caught' look again. He, too, wanted to see Rachel but Fern had forestalled him. He turned back reluctantly to Verena.

'Keith darling, you are glad I got that part, aren't you?'

He was surprised at her anxiety. 'I'm delighted,' he said sincerely.

'You are sure you don't mind me getting so involved with the stage?' she persisted. 'I mean, if this is a long run, well, I shan't be here very much. But it may be that you haven't had a chance to realise yet, how perfect the set-up will be for you. I mean, me up in London, on the stage most of the time, leaving you free for your old lab work.' She smiled tenderly at him. 'Me, I don't go for this country life stuff — show jumping and jumble sales and flower shows. And I don't think you want it either. Well, once you've inherited, who's to make you keep up all that wild social nonsense? Not me, I can assure you. I'm all for freedom for both of us. I did want you to be quite clear about that. I'm not a possessive person, you know, Keith, darling.'

Now she had said it, and she couldn't assess whether it was successful or not. Keith stood there, looking very much his most reticent self. It wasn't possible for her to realise that behind his carefully schooled 'host face' was absolute horror as he realised the import of all this. Verena wasn't just taking herself off because of a stage part she had always wanted. She was quite sure he was going to choose her for his wife, in order to inherit.

How he hated this sort of situation! At the hospital, at university, at home with his uncle, he had been the first to escape from such embarrassment. Now at last, here was something he had to face.

He braced himself and said quickly, but with unexpected firmness, 'Verena, I think we are talking at cross purposes. The problem doesn't really arise, you know. You are quite free to pursue this wonderful part you've always wanted. There will be no question of worrying about what I shall be doing, I do assure you.'

His words sounded stilted, shockingly stiff, yet he didn't know how else to couch them. He hadn't made advances to her, nor, so far as he recollected, given her any reason to believe that she was the chosen one.

Verena evidently thought otherwise. 'But Keith — ' she began, moving more closely to him, with the intention of sliding her arms up round his neck.

He took her two wrists, quickly but firmly in his own, which just prevented her from carrying out her intention, and he said, 'I have to tell you that the chances are I shan't marry anyone.'

'What do you mean? Of course you will! You have to, to inherit! Everyone knows that!' she said, angrily, but he shook his head and kept on shaking it.

'You mean, you'd let the inheritance go, just because you don't want to marry me? I don't believe it! Nobody would willingly give up all that money just because they were faced with the need to get married. Nobody could be that crazy. All that money!' she gasped.

'Money isn't everything,' he said, with the quiet anger that Rachel knew so well.

'It damn well is, you know!' Verena retorted. 'Where would you be in that lab of yours without it? What about this fantastic medical book you're supposed to be writing? And if you don't marry, you'll lose this house and your lab and the library with it. Have you thought of that?'

He shrugged. 'I've survived before, without the comfort of the house and money.'

'Where will it go, if you don't get it? Do you know?'

He wasn't going to tell her, and then

he decided that it didn't matter. 'It will go to a scientific farming concern my uncle was interested in.'

Verena smiled nastily. 'It won't, you know. That cousin of yours said she'll contest the Will, and she means it, believe me!'

Now she really had Keith's attention. 'What do *you* know about my cousin Amelia?'

Verena was triumphant. 'Darling boy,' she drawled, 'if you will go out with that Rachel and her friend, you must expect to miss unexpected visitors.'

'But the staff have instructions not to — ' he began.

'Oh, I know. Ben was doing a wonderful job of getting rid of her but I was so bored, here all on my own, that I insisted on letting her in. She was quite interesting. Especially about that daughter of hers.'

'Lydia? She didn't come too, did she?'

'No, she couldn't, darling. Why? I'll

leave that to you to find out. It should give you a lovely surprise. Well, since you won't consider me as your bride, at least let's be friends. Well no, perhaps you won't want me to see how miserable you are, married to that redhead, and under her mother's thumb. By the way, did you know that all the others in the family are in financial trouble and need the money you'll inherit to bale them out?'

He was very white round the mouth, so when he said, 'You'd better let me arrange for someone to drive you to Town,' she said, 'No, don't bother. Now I must pack, darling, and see how Fern is getting on,' and she somehow managed to walk quite firmly to the door, though quite unaccountably her ankle began to throb painfully again.

She was a little dizzy from the realisation that she wasn't going to be able to bring that money to Paul Doncaster. She wouldn't get the part without it. She must think of something. She hadn't left here yet. She must think of something. *Something*. Or someone.

She held on to the lintel of the door and closed her eyes, thinking over her past, before she met the man who was to inherit on marriage and had looked such an easy proposition. And she remembered Geoffrey Nolan, her one-time admirer, that very elderly man who was so generous with his bouquets, his dinners after the show, his gifts he showered on her. She remembered the old impatience for him and thought with sick certainty that she must put that aside now. Geoffrey Nolan would still be there, if she wanted him, and he was all she had left. And he was rich.

★ ★ ★

Keith found Fern ready packed and waiting in the library, with the door open, keeping watch for Verena. 'Fern, don't go,' he said, going in to her. 'Something's happened here today, that

I didn't know about. Where's Rachel, do you know?'

Fern shook her head and wondered if she should tell him that she had found Rachel's room empty and her few possessions gone. He would have to know sooner or later, but Fern was so afraid that if Verena found out, she wouldn't depart, but would stay and badger him.

Keith said, 'She must be around somewhere. I'll go to her room — I must find her!'

Fern stopped him distractedly, but now he had guessed something was very wrong. He strode over to Rachel's typewriter and stared at its black uncompromising cover with a look that tore at Fern's heart. It was never covered so early in the day, and propped on it was a letter from Rachel.

He tore it open and read it. After what seemed a life-time he looked up and said, in an odd voice unlike his own, 'She's gone. She's *gone*, she says,' and then in great anger, 'Did you know about this, Fern?'

'I found her room empty, just now. I went to speak to her, about me, and why I'd decided to go. Oh, Keith, I *am* so sorry. You must find her! She can't be far away. She must have gone to the station. Take the car and go and see.'

He nodded, and went without another word. He had that desperate look on his face that she had seen in the faces of other young men, when the bottom had just fallen out of their world. It was no use talking to him. No use reminding him that if Rachel had decided to go, she wouldn't be stopped. Better give him something active to do, like chasing after her, however futile the outcome might be.

Verena limped downstairs, and found Fern alone. It took all she had, to manage to look pleasant. It wasn't Fern she wanted to see, but Keith. She had thought of a way to make him change his mind. She couldn't have done it before. It wasn't the time. Her sense of timing was good, and if Keith had been there alone, she might have persuaded him, simply by letting him know what a fool he had been made of, and that his red-headed cousin had been in the house all the time, successfully making him think that she was just a grey-haired secretary and housekeeper. Verena thought she knew Keith well enough to know how angrily he would react to that, and she was quite sure that he hadn't really meant that he would give up the house to his cousin Amelia, or to some charity. It wasn't in reason.

'Where's Keith?' she demanded, and Fern said simply, 'He's gone to find Rachel. She's packed and left.'

Now Verena couldn't keep the pleasant front up. Her face blackened with anger and disappointment. 'The fool!' she stuttered. 'Wait till he finds out that her hair is normally red. Wait till he finds out that she's Lydia Lawrence. Just wait, the idiot!'

Fern felt sick. 'I think he knows that already,' she said.

Verena hadn't really believed it when Amelia had said that Lydia and Keith had trained at the same hospital. Well, if that were true, it was likely that Keith hadn't known it before. He probably went about with his thoughts on his work, not looking at anyone. He might even have been in a different part of the hospital. But she was quite sure that Rachel had known him, and that she had planned everything. She said now, 'If he knows already, it's because someone told him. You told him!'

'No. He may have guessed from something I said, but I don't think it will matter. I believe he loves Rachel and he doesn't know it. Shall we go?'

'Go where?' Verena stuttered. 'If you think I'm providing transport to town for you, you're mistaken. I'm off to find Keith!'

Fern watched her go, with a thoughtful look. She had doubted that ankle, as Rachel had, but now she wasn't so sure. Verena was in some pain from it. She called, 'I'd rest that leg, I really would, if I were you!' but that merely stiffened Verena's determination to stop Keith from finding Rachel.

Everything went wrong. Her car wouldn't start up, so she looked for something else. Ben was in the big garages talking to the chauffeur. Verena frowned. 'Hello, why weren't you driving Mr. Keith when he went off just now?' and the chauffeur looked at Ben before answering which further incensed Verena. Finally, they said, 'He didn't want to go by car. He took the horse.'

'This is no time for silly jokes!' Verena stormed. 'Where did he go?'

'Like I'm telling you, madam, he didn't want the car because he wanted to head her off, so he took the path up the hill through the woods.'

'Well, which car did she take?' Verena said, chokingly.

'She didn't, madam. She took the other horse, because of the bridle path through the woods,' the chauffeur explained, being purposely vague. He didn't like Verena either.

'And where were they both bound for?' she asked angrily.

'I'm sure I couldn't say, madam,' the chauffeur finished, and turned firmly away to finish polishing the other car.

Verena said, 'I want that car! There is some matter of importance I have to tell Mr. Keith. I must find him quickly!'

The chauffeur looked blandly at Ben and stood back. 'Very well madam, it's all ready.'

'I want you to drive me!' she stormed, baulking at an old bone of contention. None of the staff Rachel had hired for Keith ever bothered to treat Verena with the proper manner.

'Sorry, madam, that I can't do,' the chauffeur said, firmly. 'Being off duty this very instant. I understood you were a good driver. This car's no trouble!' So Verena had to take it. It wasn't auto drive and now her foot was paining her so much that if the two men hadn't been standing watching her, she would have been tempted to go back into the house and abandon her angry plan to go after Keith. But face saving was a great thing with Verena and she couldn't let these men see her return defeated to the house.

She drove steadily down the drive, and then realised she didn't know which direction to take, for this bridal path through the woods. Well, she could ask someone on the way, she supposed.

The village lay just ahead, winding and twisting, and Keith's bigger car was not easy, with an ankle in the condition of her own. She played with the idea of stopping off at the doctor's, but he would force her to abandon the trip. Finally she stopped near the village policeman, who was talking to the sexton, and asked him for directions.

'Through the woods on the horse, was she?' he asked, with great interest. He knew Rachel well, so did the sexton. 'That'll be to the Kelford place, then,' he concluded and the sexton nodded and they exchanged a significant look. 'So it's true that the wind's blowing that way,' they both said, matily.

Verena said fiercely, 'Would you mind telling me just what you mean, and also, if you can spare the time, tell me how to get there by road?'

'Oh, by road's easy enough, but of course, it's twenty miles out of your way, owing to a bit of a landslide they had recently and you being a stranger, miss — 'but Verena cut across him and demanded answers to her question.

'Well, I don't suppose it matters you knowing miss, seeing as the whole village has been taking bets on who Miss Rachel'd get — Mr. Chilton or Tom Kelford,' the policeman said with a broad grin. 'I go for Tom Kelford every time, seeing as he's a bruising rider to hounds and Miss Rachel's got a fine seat, bless her.'

'I don't want your opinion, I just want to know how to reach the Kelford property in as short a time as possible, in this car!'

The local constable was a young man, with a twitch of humour, and he didn't think a smart, well-made-up person who was also on the stage, should spoil herself by being so cantankerous, so he thought he'd teach her a little lesson, and with the able help of the sexton they guided her the longest way round, writing it down on a page torn out of his notebook, thinking it would take her best part of two hours, and that Keith and Rachel would have had time to get there and back before their disobliging guest got there.

Neither of them knew about Verena's ankle or of how it was swelling and caused her excruciating pain each time she put her foot on the clutch, and as they'd guided her on to a lonely road there was nobody to see that the car hadn't taken Barley Hill, but had gone through the fence and finished up tangled in the bushes on the edge of the river, nor that the driver had knocked herself out and was flopped unconscious over the steering wheel when darkness fell. Nor did Keith and Rachel know about it that night.

Keith didn't like riding. Rachel had taken the big bay. In the sort of mood she was in, she took the first one to hand, and the groom had had the bay out exercising it and hadn't unsaddled, as Rachel stormed into the stables. Her luggage was stowed in the boot of the other car, to be taken over to the Kelford house. It all depended on Tom now, and there wasn't really any reason, she thought, why he should have changed his mind since he had indicated that he wanted to marry her.

She was topping the rise through the woods when she heard the other horse behind her. Startled, she stopped to see who it was. Tom? There was hardly anyone else who would ride up here at this time of day.

She was shocked to see Keith. He was such a poor rider and the horse knew it. She was playing him up already, yet she was considered mild compared with the style of the bay. Rachel turned her horse's head and went back. 'What in the world are you doing?' she asked him.

Something had happened. She couldn't ever remember seeing him look so angry. 'Rachel! Why did you go off like that?' he thundered.

'I did explain in my letter,' she said slowly, not quite sure how to handle this new Keith.

'You explained nothing! You just said that in all the circumstances you felt it better to go. Go where? You didn't say! What are you doing on that uncertain-tempered brute, and why come up here? I could have understood it if you'd taken a cab to the station — but why up here?'

'Didn't Verena tell you?' Rachel asked him.

'What Verena said, has nothing to do with it. She is a very spiteful young woman and I'm glad she's going. Or didn't you know she was off with Fern, back to London? Some fool has offered Verena the part she's always wanted.'

Rachel's eyes narrowed. 'Paul Doncaster has given her a part?' She sounded so surprised and unbelieving that Keith began to wonder what was behind all this.

'Look, Rachel, for pity's sake, let's go back and sit down in a civilised way and talk. You know I hate riding — '

'I'm not going back, Keith,' she said firmly. 'No doubt Verena has come to some arrangement about money with Paul Doncaster and no doubt it's quite true that she's getting a part in his show, though I find it difficult to believe, but Fern — '

Keith never heard what she was going to say about Fern, for a small dog bounded out of the bushes, startling his horse. It reared, and Rachel's bay bolted.

There was so little room to move. The young thin trees were thick here, and it was some minutes before she could steady the bay and bring it round again, to return to where she had left Keith. There was no sign of his horse, but Keith himself lay in an awkward position, his face ashen, his eyes closed.

Rachel slid from the bay and flopped on her knees beside him. In that moment, everything she had ever learned in that brief time that she had been a nurse, fled out of her head. She knelt there numb, staring at him, and she felt in that moment that her world had crashed around her ears. Without Keith, she saw then, she had nothing left to live for.

★ ★ ★

The policeman left the sexton, and finished his duty, but the thought of Rachel riding up the hill to the Kelford estate, while that other young woman was bad-temperedly driving the car miles out of her way, intrigued him. Which of those two did she really want to have a row with, he wondered? He hazarded, at a guess, that it would be Rachel, though she had said she wanted particularly to speak to Mr. Chilton. The young policeman thought there would be no harm in his strolling up the hill. There were any number of excuses he could give for being there, although by then he would be off duty. But now it became imperative to know what was going on between those two young women and the heir of Chilton Grange. So he went up the hill, and Rachel, half running, half slithering down couldn't believe her eyes that someone like him should be anywhere near. The bay had cast a shoe so she couldn't ride it back. She had it by the bridle and she resolved never to take the brute out again, that was, if she ever got the chance.

'Whatever's happened, miss?' the young policeman asked in concern. Rachel's face was scratched, and without her glasses, her face looked young and vulnerable.

She said, on a little gasp, 'Mr. Chilton's been thrown by his horse and it made mine bolt — he's up there, unconscious!'

The most exciting thing that ever happened in his village was the odd poacher or drunk, but he knew what to do in an emergency. Rachel hadn't dared believe that an ambulance could be laid on so quickly, nor that so many willing hands could take up a hurdle to bring Keith down.

'But what beats me is,' the young policeman kept saying to his friends later, as he enjoyed a quiet half pint at the Rose & Crown, 'why she didn't go on to the Kelford house for help! She was nearer there than the village! But no, she comes all that way down to get help and the Kelfords seemingly never knew she was going there! What do you make of that?' he asked everyone, and the bets changed. It would be Mr. Chilton she was after, then, they all hazarded.

But what state would Mr. Chilton be in now, everyone asked? He had been taken to the big modern hospital in which he had stowed the children from Pond Cottages, and he had been whipped up to the operating theatre straight away. 'Touch and go,' the landlord said with satisfaction. His nephew was one of the porters at the hospital and guaranteed to keep the village posted with news. 'Concussion, head wound, busted ribs, broken leg, the lot. I wouldn't mind betting that horse of his had a go at him, while Miss Rachel was off on hers. Fancy a horse daring to bolt with Miss Rachel riding it!'

'I'd give a lot to know what happened when those two met in the woods, though,' the young policeman said thoughtfully. 'What I can't understand is, what happened to the other young woman. Went wrong after I gave her directions, I suppose. Wonder what she'll have to say when she gets back?'

'I'd keep out of sight if I was you,' the landlord advised him.

But there wasn't any need for that advice, for at that moment the telephone rang. It was the landlord's nephew, the porter at the hospital, recounting the titillating bit of news that the actress who'd been staying at

Chilton Grange, had been found at the bottom of the hill, trying to free herself from the wreckage of Keith's largest car, where she had crashed it that afternoon. She, too, had been taken to the same hospital.

10

To Keith, the hours merged into one. It was all green with a great dark animal rearing, throwing him, trampling him and trotting away, its hoof beats sounding strangely mocking in the quiet of the wood. He called to Rachel but he couldn't make her hear because his own voice couldn't be made to leave his pain-racked body. It was like in a terrible dream, where one's legs feel like cotton wool and the voice is a whisper when it should be a shout. And Rachel's horse had bolted with her.

Into the nightmare that was punctuated with the jolting of the ambulance and the brief seconds when he knew he was being taken to theatre, it became a most pressing need to have Rachel by his side, but the conviction took possession of him, that she, too, had been terribly injured that day and was probably dead. His whole existence became hinged to trying to make his voice work, to tell them he wanted Rachel. He must find out what had happened to her.

But the green of the woods seemed to smother him and when at last the green mists cleared away and he found he could make sounds, he heard her name being torn from his throat, over and over, like a mad croaking: 'Rachel! Rachel! *Rachel*!'

Someone murmured, 'We must find this Rachel. She must be sent for, if we can!' And a cool hand took his wrist and voices murmured as he went down into the green depths again.

But a little later he awoke to find Rachel sitting beside him. A thinner Rachel, looking oddly different. The random thought flashed into his mind that the difference was in some way concerning Tom Kelford. She had been going to the Kelford house that day. He knew it with a sort of uneasy conviction, and he thought he knew why.

He tried feebly to put his hand out to take hers, but couldn't so she took his hand in hers and sat holding it. But he couldn't ask her all the things he wanted to. He could feel himself slipping away again.

Dark shapes bothered him. His hospital days were repeating themselves; his aunt dying of that disease, and the need in him, the yearning, to study it, if only because of that beloved woman. But it was all mixed up with a red-headed nurse he had walked into one day, and then her face changed to Rachel's and her hair faded to grey. But every time he came up from the dream he found Rachel sitting there, although sometimes it was dark outside, and the ward lights on, sometimes the afternoon sun slanted through a window near him, hurting his eyes. And once it was a cold day, with slashing needles of rain on the windows. It came to him that these were all different times, but that Rachel was there all the time.

'Don't go,' he managed to plead, and

he heard her agree that she wouldn't.

He didn't know how long he had been there, when he finally managed to talk to her. Days of pain, another operation, too many visitors — people like Neville Shaw, all connected with work — and Rachel somehow elusive through it all, though he knew she was there. And then the fever left him and he knew he was out of danger but that only frightened him because he knew that once he was well enough to be out of that state when Rachel's presence had been imperative, she would go, and he would lose her.

It was a cold day, and he had been waiting so long for her appearance, but when she came, she walked so briskly to his bedside, and that grey hair was all hidden under a close-fitting fur cap that matched her coat, and she didn't look like his Rachel at all.

'Why didn't you come before this?' he asked her.

'I came all the time you needed me,' she said.

'But all these tiresome people, talking about business, and making me tired. Aren't you my secretary any more?'

'Neville brought his. He preferred to,' she said, tight-lipped.

Something was very wrong. It had been like this before, as if a wedge had been driven between them. 'I've wanted you,' he said. 'What's the matter, Rachel?'

'I couldn't tell you before. They said I mustn't risk upsetting you. But if you really want to know, I'm having to leave you. You know I'm not really a secretary — I'm an actress. And I've been offered a part.'

He couldn't believe it. 'I must be unconscious again,' he sighed, closing his eyes. 'I remember a day when I got a letter from you saying you were leaving me, and the sky fell in. I think I must have gone a little mad that day. Fern told me you'd gone but I couldn't believe it.'

She sat there impassively, so he said urgently, 'Don't make me talk, Rachel. I get so tired. I love you. I want to marry you!'

She sat looking at the hand she held between her own. 'No, you don't. You needed a wife, to get your inheritance.'

'I still do,' he said, in a spent voice. 'They tell me they still allow a bedside wedding, if it's really urgent. Rachel, I don't want anyone else. Only you.'

She was silent. At last, she said, 'Don't you know how long you've been in here, Keith? I don't know how to say this, but Neville said someone must tell you and they say you're on the mend, so . . . Keith, you don't need to get married any more. Time's run out, my dear. You've lost the house. Do you mind very much?'

He couldn't believe it. But not because he cared about the house now. He just couldn't believe that he had been ill for so long. 'They've been coming every day, this last week, with documents to sign, and letters. They never told me what they were. Just got my signature. And nobody told me it's too late,' he breathed.

She didn't know what to do. She had shed so many tears lately, she was so spent now, at this stage, that she felt she'd never be able to cry any more. She would have saved him this if she could, but there was no way she could have done anything. There wasn't now, anyway. He might think he loved her, but he wouldn't, when he found out.

'Keith, you're not hard up, you know. Your uncle didn't really think he'd persuade you to marry. Neville told me about it. There was a letter he had to open, on the day that the time ran out. Your uncle left you comfortably provided for; it's only the house that you don't get. But you won't be hard up.'

'Who wants money?' he said, closing his eyes.

'Well, my dear, you do, don't you, for your research?'

'No,' he said, surprised that he could bring himself to say it. 'It was what I wanted, once. And then I met you.'

'Your elderly secretary,' she said firmly.

'Oh, Rachel, don't let's play games any more,' he said wearily. 'I'm a doctor. At least, I was once. I knew there was something not quite right, but I never got down to making you tell me. It was rather . . . fascinating, playing the waiting game, I suppose. I thought one day you'd trust me and tell me why you were dressing up, playing a part. Only you never did trust me. It was Kelford, wasn't it?' He tried to turn her hand over, but when she let him at last, he found to his surprise that her fourth finger was bare.

'Yes, I was going up to tell Tom I'd marry him, that day, in the woods, only . . . ' she began feverishly, but they had let the visiting time go. She got up with regret as the bell went.

'Come again?' he pleaded.

'What's the use, my dear? You'll hate me when you know what my secret really was. Let me keep an illusion of our friendship.'

'Rachel, will you kiss me?' he whispered, still holding fast to her hand. 'Is it too much to ask?' he pressed, as he saw she was going to refuse.

She was torn both ways. She wanted to kiss him with such a rush of emotion that she didn't know how she stood there. And then footsteps pattered along the corridor, and a familiar female voice said, 'So that's who is hogging all your visiting time! They wouldn't let me come until now, but I have something to say to you, Keith,' and his cousin Amelia bustled in. 'As for you Lydia, I did think you would refrain from being so selfish, worrying me with not knowing where you were, and then letting this chance slip by, and now where are we? Does he know that he's too late to marry anyone now?'

Keith tried to sit up. 'Amelia!' he said, tensely. 'Not now. Go away!'

'Hasn't this naughty girl told you?' Amelia said, and she was by no means pleased. 'Really, I don't know what to do with someone so selfish. She *knows* what the situation is at home — '

'Don't, Mother!' Rachel said painfully. 'Leave it. It's all over. Nothing more to be done. You must see that!'

'Well, I don't! We need money as much as Keith here, and it's a shame — '

'Mother, please go!' Rachel said, looking round for a nurse.

'And he's run out of time, and he *still* gets all the money!'

The ward sister came to see what the raised voices meant, and chased Keith's visitors out, but before Rachel had reached the stairs, tight-lipped and angry, her mother still talking agitatedly about the unfair state of things, a nurse came hurrying after them and asked Rachel to go back.

'Sister says he'll be put back, he's so upset, if you don't go back and speak to him,' the nurse said. So Rachel went with her.

Keith was white as a sheet and lay back on his pillows in an exhausted way, but when he saw who it was, he said, 'My dear, it doesn't matter. I knew you were Lydia.'

She sat down because she felt her legs wouldn't support her any longer. 'You knew? *When?*' she gasped.

'Oh, some time ago. I can't recall just when. I think it was when you first got so angry that I should be unfair to someone I hadn't even spoken to. Well, of course, I had, only I didn't know she was my cousin. Don't you remember? You were a nurse at my hospital and I walked into you that day. I'd had a bad day in the lab and I wasn't looking where I was going.'

'Yes, I remember. But why didn't you say?'

'You are such a good actress, there were times when I was sure I had made a mistake. Never mind that now. Tell me, where is Fern?'

'She had to go, you know. There was a concert tour fixed. You've been ill so long.'

'And Verena?' he pressed. 'I thought I

heard someone say she was a patient in this hospital?'

Rachel hesitated, but decided to tell him about the car crash. 'She wasn't badly injured. She isn't here now. She went back to London, but your car is a write-off, I'm afraid.'

'Never mind. I don't suppose I shall be fit to drive it.'

'Keith, are you very angry with me for cheating you, acting a part and not telling you I was someone you said you hated?'

He stared at her, momentarily put off what he had wanted her to come back for. 'Is that why you went away? Is that why — ?' he murmured, frowning.

She nodded. 'That day when I was in the sun lounge, after the fire, I was going to say yes, only I remembered I mustn't because you said you trusted me implicitly and that I'd never deceive you in any way.'

He sank back on his pillow and smiled helplessly. 'Oh, my dear — what idiots we are. I'm afraid I meant deceive in the sense of being unfaithful. I knew what Verena was like, you see. I knew you weren't like that.'

He took her hands. 'Now I'm too tired to say what I wanted to. Rachel (you'll always be that, I'm afraid! Do you mind?) dear girl, will you kiss me?'

'Don't make me,' she whispered. 'I want to so much, but if I do, I won't be able to leave you.'

'That's all I wanted to hear,' he said, in wonderment.

'No, you don't, you don't,' she said wildly. 'You don't want me because where I go, the family will go. You won't want that parcel of trouble. You don't know what they're like! They're my people but you want peace, you don't want — '

'Rachel, love, I want you,' he insisted, and pulled her down to him.

She kissed him gently, but with surprising strength for an invalid, he held her to him, and kept on kissing her, with a kiss that sapped her strength and her will-power, so that she knew she would have to refuse that part she had just been offered, and that somehow, in spite of all her striving to get ahead on the stage, she no longer cared. This was what she wanted, to be with Keith, and to be loved by him.

When at last he let her go, he looked rather dazed and she said anxiously, 'Are you all right? They said I wasn't to upset you!'

'You haven't. You're good for me. I just can't believe it, that I won't ever have to face the day when I shall lose you, dear love. Oh, Rachel, if ever a man hated his solicitor, I hated Shaw when I found he was dating you. And how I restrained myself from becoming violent with young Kelford and his easy possessiveness the day he visited you, I shall never know. Rachel, you do realise we haven't got the Grange any more?'

She nodded. 'And you do realise you don't have to marry? You can stay a comfortable anti-social bachelor all your life — '

'I don't want to. I just want to be

with you.' He pulled her to him again and rested his cheek against hers. 'This is as it should be. The other wasn't right — marrying to fulfil the terms of the Will. I said when I first heard about it, how could my good uncle do that to me? No, this is as it should be. I know you love me for myself, and you know you're all the world to me, and that I don't want to live alone any more.'

Sister looked in, saw the change in her patient's face, and decided to give them a few minutes longer, now that young woman's objectionable parent had been persuaded to leave.

'What will you do, Rachel? You really want that part, don't you? Will I have to share you with the London stage?'

'No, oh no, I don't really want it. It was an ambition when I had nobody special, but now I have you, I think . . . I really think if you weren't to mind, I'd like to finish my nurse's training.'

'That seems a very good idea. We can live in. They tell me I shall be fit to go back to the lab but not to go on the wards. I shan't be much good on my legs for some time. Shall you mind?'

She shook her head, vehemently. 'We'll be a peaceful couple.'

'And your riding — you really are a good horsewoman, Rachel.'

She was horrified. 'Keith, I never want to see a horse again! I'll never get out of my mind the sight of you being thrown!'

'Oh, well, that's good,' he sighed. 'I thought that would be a very big thing I could never share with you. I never did like riding, you know.'

He touched her face, soft, and without that lined make-up he had always hated so much. 'Don't put any more stuff on this lovely skin, Rachel,' he begged. 'Ever!' And she agreed.

Then, remembering something, he pushed off the fur cap before she could stop him, and at his gasp of surprise, she said, 'Oh, well, it grows quickly, and it was hideous. So I had it dyed back to its original colour. Do you mind?'

'It's a glorious colour,' he said. 'Just

like the nurse's who haunted my dreams. Autumn gold,' he murmured. 'When will you marry me, Rachel?' he murmured.

'As soon as you like,' she promised. 'What is there to wait for? Now you don't have to choose from so many,' she teased him.

His eyes opened suddenly. 'But I *did* choose!' he protested. 'I chose you that first night in Town, when we went to the theatre and I saw you on the stage. You stopped the show!'

'Oh, I didn't. I was small fry, and it was luck.'

'Well,' he murmured, his eyes closing again, and his hand losing its hard grip on hers, 'luck or no luck, I chose you. Right from the start. Chilton's Choice,' and he gave a small chuckle. She noticed his colour was better. He was getting well, he must be, to look like this, to sound like this. As his uncle had always insisted, Keith looked frail, but he was strong. And he would get well. She eased out, happy for the first time for so long.

'Chilton's choice,' she repeated, in a soft happy voice. 'I like that. That's what I'll always be proud to be, my love!'

THE END

Other titles in the
Linford Romance Library:

THE SANCTUARY

Cara Cooper

City lawyer Kimberley is forced to take over an animal sanctuary left to her in a will. The Sanctuary, a Victorian house overlooking the sea, draws Kimberley under its spell. The same cannot be said for her husband Scott, whose dedication to his work threatens their relationship. When Kimberley comes to the aid of handsome, brooding widower Zach Coen and his troubled daughter, she could possibly help them. But will she risk endangering her marriage in the process?

NO MORE ROMANCE

Joan Warde

After the car accident which killed her fiancé and badly injured her, Claire is travelling by train to stay with her, hitherto unknown, Aunt Mary at Forresters Haven. Hoping to avoid the pity she's encountered since the accident, she's infuriated when, on the train, she meets her distant cousin, Adam Forrester, with his patronising manner. However, her Aunt Mary is kind and understanding, there's new interests to occupy her, and there's Timothy . . . but Claire wants no more romance . . .